A Weekend Affair:

The Best Way to
Get Over One Man
Is to Get on Top of Another

A Weekend Affair:

The Best Way to Get Over One Man Is to Get on Top of Another

Noelle Vella

www.urbanbooks.net

Urban Books, LLC
97 N 18th Street
Wyandanch, NY 11798

A Weekend Affair: The Best Way to Get Over One Man Is to Get on Top of Another © 2016 Noelle Vella

ISBN 13: 978-1-62286-745-5
ISBN 10: 1-62286-745-9

First Trade Paperback Printing August 2016
Printed in the United States of America

10 9 8 7 6 5 4 3 2 1

This is a work of fiction. Any references or similarities to actual events, real people, living or dead, or to real locales are intended to give the novel a sense of reality. Any similarity in other names, characters, places, and incidents is entirely coincidental.

Distributed by Kensington Publishing Corp.
Submit Orders to:
Customer Service
400 Hahn Road
Westminster, MD 21157-4627
Phone: 1-800-733-3000
Fax: 1-800-659-2436

Chapter 1

Mischelle

> Shell, what's going on? I haven't heard from you in a week. If you don't respond, I'm catching a flight to come see about you.

It was late at night and that text message would have awakened me except for the fact I wasn't asleep. I hadn't slept in almost a week. A week ago my life came unglued. A week ago, I kept telling myself that everything was all right, my family was okay. My best friend, Gabby, hadn't heard from me since then, and like any good friend, she'd started to get worried. Her texts had gone from Hey, girl, what are you up to? to Okay, Shell, something's going on. I know it. Call me, ASAP.

I wanted to call her the moment my world had come unhinged, but I couldn't. I couldn't tell her that she'd been right all along. I couldn't tell her that I should have listened to her a long time ago. No. No woman wanted to have to eat crow and admit that everyone else had seen the bad moon rising before she had. No woman wanted to admit that she couldn't see the forest for looking at the trees. But Gabby was a good friend and had been since the day I'd met her back in '07.

So I dried my tears and picked up my cell. Pressed the call button on the touchscreen and waited for her to pick up. I looked around my house—because it was no longer a home—and sighed as tears rolled down my face. The place was spotless. I'd cleaned until I couldn't clean anymore. I found I did a lot of that as of late, doing things by rote to take my mind off the shambles that had become my life. I cleaned and scrubbed away any dirt and debris just as I wished I could do my life.

"Shell?" Gabby answered on the third ring.

"Yeah," I mumbled out.

"What in God's name is going on? Where have you been?" she blurted out.

I wanted to pretend, like I'd done so many times before. Wanted to fake the funk and say everything was okay, that I'd just needed some me time. But Gabby was smarter than that. She would know I was lying before I even finished telling the lie. And to be honest, I was tired of trying to hold it all together. After all that had happened, I didn't talk to anybody because I was too ashamed. I couldn't tell my mother because, in her eyes, my husband, Malik, could do no wrong. I didn't have many friends to begin with. So through this whole ordeal, I'd had only me and my children.

I started sobbing loudly.

"Shell, what on earth . . .?" Gabby inquired.

I could hear the angst in her voice. For as long as we'd been friends she'd never heard me bawl like this.

"I caught Malik cheating on me," I confessed.

I knew that cheating was so normal these days that it felt like no one even batted a lash at it anymore. People actually found it more shocking to be faithful. That was how common cheating had become. But for me . . . for me, my tears were for so much more than the fact that my husband had cheated on me. My tears were for my children who'd become statistics by default. They were now a part of a single-mother household because my husband had decided to walk out on us. I was hurt, distraught, and scared shitless.

"What?" Gabby yelled so loudly that it scared me.

I jumped—startled—and almost dropped the phone. Tears drowned my face and blended with the mucus running from my nose. My throat felt swollen. My lips were dry, minus the tears and the snot. My tongue was heavy, and my mouth felt like cotton.

"Malik was cheating on me," I repeated, knowing Gabby had heard me the first time, then got up to pace the front room.

"I knew it," she yelled. "I knew that SOB was up to something. When you told me about—"

"He left me and the kids," I cut her off. "Took the car and now he's at the girl's house."

"Oh my God! What?"

She too had been so stunned all she could do was call on the Most High. While she screamed to the heavens and asked what, when, where, why, and how, I kept talking. I stopped myself from rambling and started from the beginning . . .

I knew something was wrong as soon as I pulled into the parking space in front of my apartment. It had been a long day, and my day had started out shitty while at school. My Introduction to Criminal Law professor had taken me through the wringer. Professor Hall was a great instructor, but he could be an asshole at times. He'd always been hard on us, but that day, he thought it pertinent to call me out on my APA citations in front of the whole class. I was pissed, embarrassed, and a little humiliated. However, those emotions had to be set to the side for the moment.

As I pulled my metallic blue 2002 PT Cruiser into the normal parking spot in front of my two-bedroom townhome, I could hear the TV blasting and my children screaming at the top of their lungs. Normally, they were quiet when my husband or I were home and watching them. They didn't carry on that way. I immediately thought something was wrong. My husband and I had been married for eight years. It hadn't always been the best, but it wasn't the worst. We'd had our ups and downs, but what relationship hadn't?

We lived in a sketchy neighborhood. No, it wasn't the hood of hoods, but it could be the hood that Boyz in the Hood warned us about, depending on the time of day and mood of things. Spanish and English seemed to coincide as different ethnicities clashed. Highland Manor on Upper Riverdale Road didn't give you a welcome home feeling, but it was my home. The bricked buildings looked as if they needed to be pressure washed. The landscaping could stand some upkeep. Mexican music and hip-hop collided, while the smell of fried chicken and a Hispanic dish fought for dominance over the air. I looked around the apartment complex to make sure nothing looked out of the ordinary. It was about four in the afternoon. January seemed as if it was on a marathon sprint as it was going by fast. It was unusually warm for the season. That should have been my first sign that something was wrong. No way it should have been that warm in winter. The sun was beaming down. Kids were outside playing, some on skates, and others on skateboards. No big coats that would have told of winter, only sweaters and sweatpants to stave off the light chill of the wind.

After hopping from the car, I rushed up the stairs leading to my door, wondering just what the hell was going on in my home. As soon as I pushed the door open, my eyes widened. My three-year-old daughter Leianni was chasing my four-year-old son Hassan around the front room. He had a cake frosting container in his hands holding it up so she couldn't reach it. They were both covered in chocolate from head to toe. The theme song to Doc McStuffins was playing so loud I could barely hear myself think. For a minute I just shook my head. Words stuck in my throat as I looked at the frosting that covered my furniture and walls.

Where in God's name was my husband? I thought as I closed the door behind me.

"Hassan, what are you two doing?" I asked as I stopped my son midrun.

"Mommy, he won't let me have none," Leianni whined.

"He won't let me have any," I corrected her.

"She keeps trying to eat it all," Hassan chimed in. "Daddy said we had to share."

I sighed heavily. Leianni's big Afro puffs were chocolate infused. Angry tears rolled down her golden-brown cheeks. Hassan had a smirk on his face redolent of the one his father would carry.

I snatched the cake frosting from him, then fussed, "You two know better than this."

"But Daddy—but Daddy said we could have it," he whined.

I had to calm down. Had to get my wits about me. My annoyance was about to make me lash out at my children when it was their father who I wanted to cuss. I dropped my purse and my keys on the end table by the couch, the table the only thing not covered in chocolate.

"Sit down," I sternly told the two. "And neither of you had better move until I get back."

My children plopped down where they stood, both with pouts on their faces. I figured Malik had wanted to get some sleep as he'd been working a lot lately and had probably told the kids they could have the cake frosting so he could close his eyes for a bit. I knew he had to be tired, but the least he could have done was stay downstairs with them. I balled my lips and rushed up the stairs. The heels on my feet needed to come off because my ankles were screaming, but I ignored the pain for the moment.

I probably looked like Miss Sophia as I barged up the carpeted stairs, but it was very irresponsible on my husband's part to leave the kids unattended. I could hear Miguel's "Quickie" playing. So not only was he asleep, he had music on so he couldn't hear what was going on with our children downstairs too? I tried to open the door to find it locked so I entered the bathroom through the hall since our room was connected to the bathroom. I took a quick glance at the mess of Malik's clothes littering the bathroom floor and shook my head. No matter how much I cleaned, he would still be a messy man.

He wasn't the cleanest man in the world, but I'd dealt with worse from him and survived it. I could have sworn I heard Malik talking to someone. If he was on the phone and not sleeping, then why would he leave the kids downstairs like that, I wondered. It may have sounded crazy, but as soon as my hand touched the doorknob, a chill settled in my spine.

I twisted the knob to my bedroom and got the shock of my life.

"Ah, yeah, girl. Take this dick," Malik grunted out.

His head was thrown back, the ends of his braids hanging down his back as the muscles in his ass strained with each pump. In front of him was a dark brown—hairy—ass that didn't belong to me. Her long weave fanned across her toes as it swooshed and swayed.

"Damn," she breathed out. "Shit, that's the spot, nigga," she crooned.

In that moment, it was like the world stood still. Things that didn't even matter stood out to me. My bed was in disarray. Red down comforter had been thrown to the floor. Pillows were scattered about. A woman's black panties with white crust in the seat were atop of one of them. Malik's drawers were hanging around his left ankle. The cream blackout panels were blowing in the wind of the ceiling fan. My closet door was open. Malik's shoes tumbled out like he had been searching for something.

His dick was glazed with her satisfaction, and her vagina was making a weird noise. It sounded like he was stirring macaroni. I didn't even notice the smell. He wasn't wearing a condom. I noticed that. My husband's dick was pushing in and out of another woman, and there was no condom separating them. I didn't know what came over me, didn't know if it was anger or rage. Couldn't tell if I had snapped or if I was floating outside my body. What I did know? I knew I picked up the lamp sitting on the dresser by the door, and I cracked it right upside my husband's face.

His mistress screamed, and then fell to the floor trying to grab something to cover her bouncing breasts. My husband yelled out as the ceramic drew blood.

"You must be out of your goddamned mind to be in my house with my children downstairs fucking another woman!"

I heard the words, but I didn't know the woman speaking. It was like someone else had taken over me. All I could think about was all the shit Malik had taken me through. I thought about how I had to deal with his ex-girlfriend. I remembered the nights I cried as I held our three-month-old son in my arms and wondered where he was. I remembered those times he claimed to be playing ball or in the studio, only to find out he'd been with his ex. I thought back to how we had to fight to get back on solid foundation, how the pain and hurt had kept me awake at night. There was nothing that could take away the knots in my stomach because I knew he was out cheating on me.

And then there were the apologies. The times he'd cried with his head on my lap, promising me that it had all been a mistake and that he would never take us through that again. Then came the second pregnancy, followed by the marriage. Even after all of that, I'd tricked myself into thinking that he would be a man of his word. Forced myself to overlook the times when he verbally and mentally abused me. I pushed to the back of my mind the times when he'd become so angry he would punch holes in the walls, kick doors down, and get in my face like we were combatants on the street.

I remembered the fights and the yelling. Remembered the way he would tell me I was crazy because I questioned him. I questioned his whereabouts at times because I had this nagging feeling in my gut that told me Malik had been up to his old tricks. My dreams had started to haunt me. They showed me my husband's adulterous ways, but I'd ignored them. Why? Because I didn't want to be a single mother. For the sake of my children, I put on a façade like I had the perfect marriage.

Malik and whoever the bitch was cowering in the corner had taken all that away from me. As I launched at my husband, kicking and screaming like a wild banshee, that whore sat in the corner screaming and crying.

"Yo, Shell, chill," Malik roared at me.

Blood was in his eyes as he tried to get ahold of me. But my anger couldn't be contained. With ease, I kicked him in his dick, then sent a rapid succession of slaps and punches to his face and body as he fell down. My braids fell down from their neat bun as I stomped him. He kept sliding further and further underneath the bed to shield himself from my wrath. For as long as we'd been together, Malik had never seen this side of me. To him, I seemed docile, I knew it. Because I'd let him beat me into the ground with his words, he never knew that I possessed the level of anger I was bestowing on him.

I'd forgotten my children were downstairs. Had forgotten my senses as I picked up the radio and threw it at the bitch in the corner. The CD portal on top of the small radio popped open when it landed in her face. She screamed, and then tried to get up. Feet spread shoulder-length apart, I yanked her from the corner by her precious weave. The butt whupping I was laying on her no doubt looked like something from the hood in a Worldstar Hip-Hop fight video, but I didn't care. The fact that I had two degrees and was working on a third didn't matter. As my arms swung back, and then came forward to land my fists in her face, I cared about nothing.

Tears stung my eyes as I wailed on her, then threw her head into the opened closet door.

"Shell, chill," Malik called out behind me.

How dare he tell me to chill! My hand was tangled in messy weave. His fuck toy had clawed my face and neck as she struggled to get footing in the one-sided brawl. Malik grabbed me from behind. Because of his intrusion, the girl got in a few hits to my face, which only pissed me off further. I pulled my hand free from its weaved entanglement, bucked and kicked my legs like a windmill, sending the end of my heels into the girl's face.

"Let me go," I screamed.

Malik tossed me on the bed and held me there as he yelled at Janay—I now knew her name—to leave.

"Go, just go," he yelled at her while pinning me down on the bed.

Blood trickled down the side of his face onto my chest. Janay snatched up her clothes—bitch left her filthy panties—and hightailed from my bedroom.

I came back to the present as I told Gabby the whole sordid tale.

"Shit just got worse from there," I said. "He and I continued to fight. My kids had to see and hear all of this. I lost it, Gabby. I just lost it. In my house, in our room, with our children downstairs. He had no regard for me, no respect for our children, or our marriage."

"That's a dirty—and I'm sorry, I'm just gonna say it—nigga. That's a dirty damn nigga."

Gabby's words shocked me. She normally didn't use any kind of profanity or use the N-word.

"It gets worse," I kept going.

I looked out the blinds of my front window. Darkness engulfed my home, but it was bright and shiny on the outside world. Real life depicted my mood. I smiled and fronted on the outside for my children; on the inside, I was a mess.

"Oh God, what else happened?" Gabby wanted to know.

"After all of that, after all that shit, he left. Took the car and left. I haven't been able to get the kids to school on time. Hassan has to be at school by seven forty-five. Malik doesn't come to the house until about eight fifteen. He's talking about going back to New York. And that's not the worst part."

"Can it get any worse, Shell? I mean, really. Girl . . ."

She sounded as exasperated as I felt.

"He doesn't work at Anna's anymore. He hasn't worked there in about three weeks. The car note hasn't been paid. My electricity has been cut off."

"But didn't you give him your school refund to take care of all this stuff?"

I nodded as if she could see me. The tears had stopped, but the ache and hollowness I felt hadn't.

"I did. Apparently, he's been buying her dinner and leaving flowers on her doorstep. Bought her a new bedroom set and all."

"How—what? How do you know this?"

"Janay told me."

"So you're talking to this trash-box hooker?"

"I called her. Asked her how long all this had been going on."

"And she told you?"

"Yeah."

"Oh, goodness, I'm so sorry, Shell. Where are the kids?"

"They're at Renee's for now."

"And what did she have to say about all this?"

I sighed inwardly, thinking about my mother. I called her by her first name because I didn't feel she deserved the title mother, mom, or mama. There was long, tainted history between my mother and me, and it showed in the way we regarded each other.

"She asked me what I'd done to make my husband feel he needed a mistress."

Gabby made a sound that said she was disgusted. "Ugh, I have no comment. That's your mother, so I have no comment, but you already know how I feel. Give me the information to your power company."

"Gabby, I already owe you money."

"Shell, this isn't the time to be prideful, okay? Give me your information and let me take care of this for you. You can be prideful later. You need your kids home with you. God forbid Malik tries to pull some shady crap and take the kids to that chick's house."

I wanted to fight her on the matter, I did. But she was right. It was my pride making me feel like I shouldn't take the help from her. After I told her what she wanted to know, I sat in silence as she went online and paid the over three hundred-dollar bill in full. I didn't know what would happen after all this. Had no clue how to proceed. All I kept thinking was, this kind of thing doesn't happen in real life. It only happened in Tyler Perry and Lifetime movies. Apparently, my life had taken on a Perry production with a Lifetime turn of events.

Chapter 2

Gabrielle

I couldn't believe what Shell had told me. Scratch that; I *totally* believed it. What I couldn't believe was that she actually came clean about it. I mean, what woman would want to admit to something so horrible, something that she had been warned about ad nauseam. I admit, I had beat the topic into the ground, made it known on the regular that I thought Malik was cheating on her. But in my defense, Shell had given me more than enough ammunition to think the worst of Malik. And when it was all said and done, I was right, although, after hearing the sadness and despair in Shell's voice, I wished I had been wrong.

Not only had that trifling, no-account loser beat her down mentally and emotionally, but now one could add desecration, humiliation, and abandonment to his long list of marital crimes. Bad enough he was cheating on Shell, but to do it in her home, in the bed they shared, with her children right downstairs—that was just vile. I was disgusted just thinking about it. She'd probably hate me for this, but I thought the best thing Malik ever did for Shell was leave.

Yes, I hated the fact that he basically left her and their children destitute, with no funds saved for her financial security and with only occasional royalty checks from her books that she had written, but he was dead weight who contributed very little to the household to begin with. It may not seem that way right now, but in the long run, she would be better off without him.

Understandably, Shell had sunken into a deep depression, and there was nothing I could do to get her out of her own head, not over the phone anyway. Over the next few days, we still talked on the phone daily, but much of the time, she would zone out on me, lost in her own thoughts. Which was why, after a week of her mood swings, I couldn't take it anymore and suggested we get away for a few days.

Not only would the trip allow Shell to vent all her frustrations in person, but it would also give me time to gain perspective, unclutter my own life, and clear my head from all the chaos around me. A hectic job, an ex who was going off the rails, and I was more than ready for some much needed me time. The plan was to kick back, check out the sights, soak up some local culture, then return home renewed and refreshed. At least, that's what I had hoped.

Let me back up for a minute to properly introduce myself. My name is Gabrielle. I currently reside in North Carolina, although at heart, I was still a true-blue city girl from Brooklyn, New York. What prompted me to move, you might ask. The simple answer: the cold weather back home had gotten the better of me. The real answer: I finally realized how stagnant I was in my job. Working as a pediatrician was nice, but it just wasn't fulfilling anymore. I realized I needed to do more with my life. That's when my then boyfriend, Daniel, and I packed everything up and moved down South a little over five years ago looking for a change of scenery and a warmer climate.

Careerwise, my life was on the upswing. A year before moving, I started applying for several sports medicine fellowships. I was lucky enough to secure a one-year fellowship at the University of North Carolina-Chapel Hill. Once that was completed, I began working at a well-known sports medicine center in the Raleigh-Durham-Chapel Hill area. I had finally found my true calling, and I was loving every minute of it.

My relationship, on the other hand . . . Let's just say it crashed, burned, and disintegrated much like the Hindenburg. The first few years were pretty good, but as time passed, I felt more and more unfulfilled. For starters, Daniel was about as affectionate as a cold, dead fish floating in the Arctic. Anytime I initiated any type of display of affection, such as a hug or a kiss, his standard response to me would be, "You're freaking me out." *Seriously?* Who does that? Not to mention his idea of intimacy was telling me to go into the bedroom and pull my panties down. I was so turned off by him that I hadn't slept with him in six months.

Any time I voiced my concerns, he made me feel like I was asking too much from our relationship, and yet, all I wanted was the *basics*; to feel loved and respected, like I actually mattered. One day, after twelve long, wasted years of settling and being unhappy, I decided I wanted out. I knew the relationship was going nowhere. No chance of marriage, no chance of children, no chance of anything. And I wanted to go somewhere—just not with him. When it was all said and done, I broke things off with Daniel, and while it felt good to finally be free, it was also terrifying. I spent most of my adult life being in a relationship, and now I had to start over; problem was, I didn't know how, and honestly, I wasn't sure I wanted to.

After the breakup, I buried myself in work, mainly, so I wouldn't have to deal with my pathetic lack of a social life. Unfortunately, I was basically a homebody and had very few friends in the state, which meant when I was home,

I had nothing but time on my hands to contemplate my depressing existence. While I had a great career, the rest of my life was in a very sad state of affairs.

Worst still, as a constant reminder of my relationship failings, Daniel refused to accept the fact that we were over. It started with constant phone calls to both my home and cell phones at all hours of the day and night, begging me to take him back. It had gotten to the point that I was forced to block his number on both phones. When his phone calls failed to sway me, he began cyber stalking me, creating fake people via e-mail and Facebook to harass and threaten me, trying to make it seem as if I needed his protection.

Little did he know, I was more cyber savvy than he gave me credit for, tracing the e-mails back to him. I had half a mind to call the police on him, but I didn't want to be responsible for sending another black man to jail, although Shell was all for it. Instead, I confronted Daniel about his antics. Of course, at first, he denied everything, but when I showed him proof about the e-mails, he eventually came clean and promised to back off. Because he seemed so sincere, I eventually unblocked him.

Finally, I thought to myself, my life can get to some semblance of normalcy, and I was going to enjoy every minute of it. That's when I decided I needed a well-earned vacation. I could have easily scheduled a trip back home, but since I was already going back for the Christmas holidays, I wanted to go someplace new and different. I talked to Shell, and she suggested Tybee Island, Georgia.

"I've never heard of Tybee Island. Where is that exactly?" I questioned.

"It's about a five-hour drive from the Atlanta airport, or forty minutes if you fly into Savannah," she replied. "When are you going on vacation?"

I had already scheduled my vacation for February. While it was technically wintertime, the state of Georgia was notorious for having unseasonably warm weather at that time of the year. And it was off-peak season, meaning the rental rates would be much cheaper. My timing now seemed like fate, considering everything that was going on with Shell.

"I have the first two weeks of February off."

"That's perfect," she noted. "The Savannah Black Heritage Festival will be going on, and I think you'd love it."

Shell spent the next five minutes telling me all about the festival, how it ran for almost the entire month of February, and about the activities that took place. She really didn't need to convince me. I was already sold.

"Do you think you can get away for a few days?" I asked.

You could hear a pin drop as I waited for her to respond. I knew Shell was wallowing and wasn't really up for a good time, but she needed this trip just as much as I did. And although she was reluctant to leave her kids for a few days, even she knew she needed a break.

Finally, sighing, she replied, "I'm not sure. You know my money situation. Besides, I'm not sure I'll be feeling up to it. I can't make any promises, but I'll see what I can do. I'm due a royalty check in a few days, so I might be able to swing it."

"And what you can't cover, I've got the rest. As far as you not feeling up to it, all I'm asking you to do is show up. I'll handle everything else." I wasn't giving her the option of backing out.

The only other issue left to address was who was going to watch her kids for the few days she was away, being that her childcare options were very limited. She had very few family members in her area, and the ones she did have were either not reliable or were not the most altru-istic. Any help she received always came with conditions. And she definitely wasn't going to ask Malik to watch the kids, especially because he was staying with his side ho.

"Shell, I hate to bring this up, but the kids—"

"You already know," she replied, cutting me off. "I'll have to ask Renee, and there's no telling what she'll say or what she'll want in return."

I shook my head in disgust. I couldn't understand how a grandmother could treat her own grandchildren so callously. Then again, her mothering skills left a lot to be desired. Shell's relationship with Renee was strained at best, estranged at worst. But considering the alternatives, Renee was her best bet. Despite her shortcomings, Leianni and Hassan adored her.

"Well, ask her anyway. You're taking this trip no matter what," I stated firmly.

"Yes, Mom," she laughed. Shell knew better than to argue with me.

As luck would have it, Renee was in an agreeable mood and said she would watch the kids. Of course, she wanted some cash to do it, but it was a small price to pay for Shell's peace of mind.

Fast-forward and here I was, the evening before the trip. I had some obsessive-compulsive tendencies, so I made sure that, aside from my toothbrush and some other essentials, I was packed at least two days prior. I took a nice hot shower around nine o'clock, planning to go to bed a bit earlier than usual since I had a very early flight.

Being a chronic insomniac, sleep was precious to me, so imagine my annoyance as I was awakened in the mid-dle of the night by someone obnoxiously banging on my door. My annoyance quickly turned to sheer revulsion when I looked through the peephole seeing who it was.

For two months, Daniel had actually stayed true to his word. That was . . . until now. He was pleading for me to let him in. I was afraid someone was going to call the police, so I reluctantly complied.

"What do you want, Daniel?" I asked, clearly vexed at him for interrupting what little sleep I had gotten.

"I need you," he slurred, trying to hug me. He smelled like a distillery. "You're all I have left."

I backed away from him, rubbing my palms down the front of my face. "Daniel, I don't know what's going on, but we're not together anymore. Ergo, you don't have me." My eyes were beginning to burn from lack of sleep, only adding to my irritation. "I'm really tired, so whatever you have to say, please just say it and go."

"G, I lost my job. You're the only good thing I have left in my life." He fell to his knees, tears in his eyes.

I sighed knowing I was probably about to make a huge mistake. "Daniel," I said, reaching my hand out to him, "please get up."

Sometimes I was a big softy, and right now, I was having one of those moments.

He took my hand, slowly getting to his feet, stumbling slightly. "I don't know what to do now, G."

I led him into the living room over to my oversized black velvet touch couch.

"Just relax, while I make you some coffee so we can talk," I said walking into the kitchen.

I wasn't a coffee drinker myself, but I always kept some on hand for guests. I pulled the container out of the cabinet, placing two teaspoons in a mug, then I added some water and put the mug in the microwave for one and a half minutes. During that time, I went to check on Daniel. When I reached the living room I noticed he was knocked out. I was jealous. It was always so easy for him to get to sleep, and stay asleep. Shaking my head, I walked over to my linen closet, fishing out a blanket. I took it back to the couch and covered him with it. I then turned out all the lights, taking my weary self to bed for what little time I had left.

Despite being bone tired, I was still excited about my trip. Nothing, or no one, was going to ruin that for me. I got ready, packing the few items I still needed for my trip. I had scheduled a cab the night before, and it was supposed to arrive in fifteen minutes. I carried my knapsack and carry-on bag to the foyer, leaving them by the front door. Then I walked into the living room to get Daniel up. He looked horrible, and he still smelled of tequila.

"Wake up, Daniel," I said, gently tapping him on the shoulder.

He slowly began to stir. "What's up?" he uttered, looking dazed and confused.

"You don't remember?"

"Remember what?"

I glanced at my watch, knowing that the cab would be arriving in ten short minutes. I needed to get Daniel out of my place so I could lock up. "Long story short, you showed up at my door drunk as a skunk crying about how you lost your job. Then you fell asleep."

He sat up slowly, clearly hungover. "Damn, I don't even know how I got here."

"I'm guessing you drove yourself. Not smart, by the way," I said, glancing at my watch, trying not to seem impatient. I actually felt bad for him about the whole job situation.

Daniel looked as if a lightbulb had turned on. "You're up early. Going somewhere?"

"Actually, I am. And I really need to be outside when this cab shows up."

"Where are you going?" he asked nosily.

"Away for the weekend," I replied.

"That's not what I asked you."

So much for feeling sorry for him.

"Well, that's all the response you're going to get." My patience was really starting to wear thin.

"Oh, so you can't tell me where you're going now? You must be going away with some nigga. That's why you won't tell me."

I hated when he used that word. If it wasn't for the fact that I was running out of time, I would have let this war of words continue, being one to not back down from a verbal fight. As it stood, my home phone rang. It was the cabdriver, letting me know he was out front. I quickly squashed what could have potentially become a huge argument.

"We're not together anymore, Daniel, so who I spend time with is really none of your concern. But since you're being so nosy, I'm going to Tybee Island for the weekend with Shell. We're going to the Savannah Black Heritage Festival. That was my cab calling, so you need to go. Now."

Slowly, he rose up from the couch, and I ushered him toward the front door. "Wow, I'm surprised that nigga of hers actually let her out of lockdown," he said, venom in his tone.

He had no clue what was going on with Shell or her broken marriage, and I wasn't about to share. Not taking him on, I grabbed my bags, secured my house alarm, and locked the door behind me. The cabdriver was already standing outside of his vehicle. He grabbed my carry-on, placing it in the trunk.

Turning briefly to Daniel, I said, "Bye," then climbed into the backseat of the cab as he stood there, a look of frustration on his face.

The cab arrived at Delta's terminal in no time flat, and I quickly made it through security with plenty of time to spare. I was glad when the gate agent called for general boarding because my eyelids were beyond heavy. Once I boarded the plane, I slid into my seat, dozing off for the entire flight—despite a crying baby and a guy with body odor so offensive, he made you want to cry.

I sent Shell a text as soon as the plane touched down at the airport in Atlanta. Even though we were still a few hours away from our destination, I already felt some of my stress of the previous few hours fading. I felt even better when I saw Shell waiting for me at the terminal entrance.

Shell was a few inches taller than I, standing at five feet seven inches. She was what one would consider a thick chick; hips, boobs, and booty for days. She often complained that she felt fat and didn't feel attractive, but I think Malik had a lot to do with that. She had a rich dark mahogany complexion, and her jet-black hair was braided with thick extensions that hung down to the middle of her back. She wore a blue and white ombré off-the-shoulder top, with dark denim capris, and white wedge sandals. The entire ensemble was quite flattering.

"Gabby!" she exclaimed, arms outstretched for a hug.

"Shell!" I replied, hugging her in return. People were staring, but we didn't care.

"How was your flight?" she asked as we boarded the shuttle bus headed for the rental car office.

"Fine, if you like crying babies and body odor that smelled like onions," I replied, a frown on my face. "If this trip wasn't so last minute, I definitely would have gone first class."

"Eeewww! That sucks," she laughed. "Bet you won't make that mistake again."

"You'd easily win that bet," I chuckled. "Kids all settled?"

Shell rolled her eyes. "Yeah. I paid Renee a hundred and fifty bucks for the weekend. That didn't include the food, snacks, and drinks I packed for my kids."

"Humph. Paying a grandmother to watch grandkids who she hardly ever sees even though you only live a few miles away . . . Not to mention all you do for her to begin with. Yep, she's a real winner." I could have said a lot more considering all I knew, but I refrained, not wanting to bring the mood down.

It didn't take us long to secure our vehicle, a black-on-black Dodge Journey, and be on our way. During the drive to Tybee Island, after briefly discussing our issues with the men in our lives, Shell and I kept the rest of our conversation light, with talk turning to the festival, Tybee Island nightlife, and our choice of location. For several days, I'd researched many possible rental properties for our weekend getaway. We wanted someplace affordable that was directly on the beach. We finally settled on a beach house called Almost Heaven. From the pictures we viewed online, it was just what we were looking for.

Around noon, we arrived at our destination, stopping first at the rental office to pick up the keys and garage door opener. When we drove up to the house, both our mouths dropped open. The beach house was a beautiful white, three-story structure with a huge two-car garage. I opened it, quickly parking our vehicle inside. Closing the garage door, Shell and I exited the SUV, gathered our respective belongings, and headed inside up the stairs leading to the main living area. Let me just say, the pictures did *not* do it justice. The inside was enormous. We left our bags in the foyer so we could explore before getting settled.

The first thing we noticed was the color scheme, with various shades of blue and cream prevalent throughout the home. The living room was expansive, containing two queen sleepers, several chairs, a coffee table, a rattan set with a table and two chairs, a 52-inch wide-screen television, DVD player, a gas log fireplace, and hardwood floors. Double doors led to the wrap-around screened porch with a six-person hot tub. Off of the living room was the supersized kitchen, which boasted a large center island, dual sink, numerous cabinets, and an eight-person casual dining area with a spectacular view of the beach.

On the same floor were two guest bedrooms, and a spare bathroom. But the pièce de résistance were the two exquisite ocean view master bedrooms, one on the second floor, the other on the third. Each contained a king-size bed, two nightstands, a couch, a desk with a chair, a chest of drawers, 42-inch television, a DVD player, a gigantic master bathroom with a whirlpool garden tub, and a sundeck with a two-person hot tub.

Looking at our surroundings, I wished we had made reservations for longer than a weekend. It would be quite easy to lose myself in a place like this. Compared to our own private hell, this house was definitely the little slice of heaven we both needed.

Chapter 3

Mischelle

After fawning over the house, getting unpacked, and settled in, the first thing we did was look for something to eat. We were starving, and Gabby got a little funky in the attitude area if she didn't eat when her body called for it. So after some Internet surfing, we settled on trying Sundae Café. It was a family-owned restaurant that catered to the romantic side of things for dinner, but their lunch specials looked mouthwatering as well.

The outside of the place was a plain brown brick building with a simple red and white sign boasting its name. The inside was nothing to write home about either. Brown wooden chairs sat against mocha-colored carpet with black-and-white checkered tablecloths on square tables. And the bar area looked as if the wood needed to be repolished. Other than that, the place had a very friendly and welcoming atmosphere.

I kept it simple and ordered fish and grits with coleslaw, hush puppies, and a drink. Gabby settled on the Smokehouse turkey burger with Carolina BBQ sauce, applewood bacon, and crispy onions. We took our food to go so we could enjoy our lunch on the sundeck overlooking the beautiful beach.

The deck was gated from the side, but you could see the white sandy beach and see the waves wash ashore. The water in the pool looked warm and inviting, but we didn't want to get in yet.

"So, now what?" I asked after we finished stuffing ourselves. "What should we get into first?"

"I figure tomorrow we can get up early and check out the activities for the festival. I printed some stuff out we may want to do," Gabby said as she walked inside to grab her laptop, then walked back out.

Gabby had always been one who had to have everything planned to the last dotted I and crossed T; otherwise, she wouldn't be able to function. I nodded as I stood and walked to look over the gate. Everything seemed so peaceful. Seagulls flew overhead. I could hear a woman's flirty laughter in the distance. Looking down, I saw her being chased by a man with an even bigger grin on his face. I smiled at the love in the air. It made me miss my husband and kids.

I felt my emotions taking over again. Just thinking about the way my husband had behaved was enough to make my eyes water. I glanced back at Gabby to make sure she wasn't watching me. Luckily, she was on her laptop looking at something. I knew Gabby had brought me here to take my mind off of things, but I couldn't help but think if I had caused Malik to cheat on me. I wondered if I could have been a better wife or something. Anything that would tell me why my husband would cheat on me, in our home.

What kind of man would disrespect his wife and kids like that? I didn't get it. Didn't understand the method to his madness. How did we get to this point?

"I'm going to use the restroom right quick," I told Gabby.

She looked up with a smile, then nodded before going back to clicking away on her laptop. I walked through the spacious kitchen, bypassed the bathroom, and then headed to get my cell. As soon as I picked it up, the bottom of my stomach fell out. Malik had called me four times. I wasn't sure I was even ready to talk to him, to be honest. What would I say?

I pressed the call button by his number and waited. Those four rings seemed to be the longest I'd ever waited. With each ring, my heart swelled under my rib cage. Before I'd left to go to the airport, Malik and I had been fighting like enemies instead of husband and wife. I screamed and yelled. He yelled and became defensive, refusing to answer my demands to know why. Why would he do this to me?

I didn't understand it, and I didn't ever think I would. How could he leave our home and go play house with a woman he barely even knew? We had eight years, *eight* fucking years under our belts! We had two damn kids! How dare he do this to me—to us! As the phone rang, the tears I tried to keep at bay angrily rolled down my burning cheeks.

Why had he called me? Did he want to try to fix our marriage? Was I *willing* to fix our marriage? What would he say to me when he answered the phone? When Malik was mad, he had the tendency to be venomous with his words. He could make me feel lower than low with his verbal assaults. To be honest, I could be a firecracker with words too, but at this point, I just didn't have any fire left in me. I was broken.

Malik didn't answer.

I ran a hand through my braids as I sighed. I didn't know what to do besides try to call him back later. I laid my phone down and thought back, trying to figure out where it had all gone wrong. Things had been tight financially as of late. To be honest, if Gabby hadn't been covering the cost of food while here, I'd probably be assed out. I'd squeezed enough money from my financial aid to cover the cost of rooming.

That was why I had enough to help with gas for the drive with a little left over. Anyone who'd ever been in a long-term relationship or marriage knew what it was to have a financial strain come in and wreak havoc. Still, I'd been the ever-dutiful wife. I did everything in my power to help my husband stand. He didn't want me to work outside the home, so I made sure to stay in school so I could get those refund checks.

I made sure to write until my fingers ached so I could get advances and royalty checks. And I only got a royalty check if the publishing gods saw fit to be nice to me that quarter. Most people would think being a traditionally published author meant you had made it. I was here to tell them their thought process was a delusion. The car note had fallen behind last month. Electricity was threatened to be cut off. Car insurance had expired. We had been in a real bind. So my refund check from school had come right on time. Shit, I still owed Gabby at least $800 from when she had helped me out months before.

The fights about money and bills had been never-ending. The sex was barely there, and when it was, I was left so unfulfilled that it had started to feel like I was letting Mister climb on top of me and handle his business.

As I was walking back down the stairs, Gabby was coming up. She had a big smile on her face so I plastered one on mine too. I didn't want to bring her mood down.

"Everything okay?" she asked.

I lied. "Yeah, after I used the bathroom, I wanted to talk to the kids. Make sure they were okay. You good?" I asked with faux jubilance. "Daniel isn't call stalking you, is he?"

She waved and laughed heartily. "Girl, no. But listen, I was looking up the nightlife around here and found this jazz spot called The Treble Cleft."

"Why, when you say cleft, I think of Michael Jackson's chin?" I asked with mock seriousness.

She chuckled as we both headed back down. "You're so foolish. I was coming up to see if you'd be up for a night on the town. And don't say no either. I can see that frown forming on your face and a ready-made excuse on your lips," she quipped with a laugh. "You need this, Shell . . ."

"Gabby, you know I don't do clubs," I whined.

"This isn't one of those kinds of clubs. It's a jazz club. Mature setting and atmosphere. Not that jump-around-N-word-throwing-pants-sagging-booty-clapping-type place."

I was chuckling so hard that she could barely finish talking for laughing too. We walked to the front room. While she grabbed her laptop to show me the club, I opened the glass sliding door so some of the cool breeze could saunter in. Gabby kicked off her shoes, then folded her legs underneath her as she sat on the chocolate couch.

The décor of the room had a chic feel. The blue and cream-toned color scheme consisted of teal, aquamarine, turquoise, sapphire, egg shell, ecru, and splatters of off-white. The main walls were cream, while an accent wall was teal. The picture on the accent wall encouraged us to live, laugh, and love in black lettering, while the backdrop boasted of dark and light blue with specks of white.

I plopped down beside Gabby and looked at the website for The Treble Cleft on her laptop. I had to admit, the place looked lively from the photos posted. People were all smiles and laughs as they danced and snapped their fingers. A mixture of races and ages dressed in cosmopolitan attire decorated the pages. The establishment tooted its own horn by calling itself "The place for grown folk to be." I was shocked to see it also had a five-star restaurant. So we'd be able to eat well and enjoy good music.

"Tonight, it says a band by the name of Roses is opening up for Something For The People," she told me.

"Oh my gosh! You mean the old nineties group?" I asked, trying to keep the cheer in my voice I didn't really feel.

"You got it."

We both broke out into a chorus of their old song. Hands in the air and snapping fingers alike. For the next few minutes, we kept scrolling through the website. Checked out their social network footprint. After a while, we decided that it was the place for us to be. While Gabby spoke of her excitement, as much as I tried to stop it, my emotions got the better of me again.

"Oh my God," I muttered.

"What?" Gabby asked, looking up from the laptop.

"It just hit me . . . that my marriage is quite possibly over."

She saw my tears, and the empathy she had for me showed on her as she frowned and reached out to hug me. "I'm so sorry, Shell. I really am."

I broke down. "I know you want to say I told you so—"

"No, no. Absolutely not. I'm not here to beat you down any more than you already are. You cry, Shell. Cry for as long as you want. Get it all out, baby."

Gabby sat there and rocked me back and forth in her arms like I was her child. She didn't judge me. Didn't say anything. She just held me, and I cried for my marriage. Shed tears for my children who could quite possibly lose their two-parent home. I cried for the loss of my best friend, my husband who I never saw leaving me. I never would have thought Malik would have walked away from our marriage or our children. I didn't know the man Malik was right now.

After a long while, I dried my tears. "I'm sorry," I told Gabby. "I don't mean to suck the life out of this weekend."

"It's okay, girl. Go ahead and get it out now. It's best you don't keep it in," she assured me. "But, what I want you to do is, go upstairs, get dressed, and let me try to take your mind off your adulterous husband and that streetwalker he cheated on you with."

I gave a light chuckle, even though I didn't want to. I nodded. "Okay."

I got up and headed upstairs. As I showered and took care of my hygiene regimen in solace, Gabby was in her room, no doubt getting dolled up. I decided to wear wide-legged black slacks that hugged my hips, along with a sheer black blouse which tapered to my waist. Underneath was a black push-up bra showcasing my D-cup breasts. I donned silver accessories to set off my ensemble. Black and silver six-inch pumps elongated my legs and thighs. I pulled my long braids up into a high bun. No makeup and a bit of plum lip gloss finished the look.

I know it seemed plain, but I loved what I saw when I looked in the mirror, especially since I normally hated looking at myself. I turned side to side and smiled despite my sullen mood. I was all set to go. We were leaving early since the show was set to start at eight. We wanted to get good seats and be close to the small dance floor in case we decided to cut a rug.

Once dressed, I decided to go downstairs and wait for Gabby. I flipped the channels on the TV, paying close attention to the weather.

"While the Black Heritage Festival continues this week-end, a bout of bad weather may halt all outside activities," the local meteorologist informed me, *"and thunderstorms and scattered showers are set to roll in later on tonight, then taper off until late tomorrow afternoon. So keep those umbrellas and ponchos ready . . ."*

I looked up as I heard Gabby coming down the stairs.

"Wow," I said with a smile. "Look at you!"

She had on a lavender spaghetti-strapped dress that stopped midthigh, showing off the time she spent in the gym and at home working out. The low V-cut made her breasts look inviting. She was a little lax in the hips department, but her ass more than made up for it, which was why the hem of the dress swooshed and swayed as she Naomi Campbell walked into the front room. Teardrop diamond earrings dangled from her ears. A matching choker and bracelet sat out on her brown skin like beacons. She had on four-inch heels that accentuated her calves and thighs. The cuffs around the ankles sparkled with faux diamonds, making her appear runway ready. She asked me to pin a few of her locs up before we'd gotten dressed. While some had been left to hang down in the back, most were up into a neat bun with a few shorter ones hanging like spirals around her face.

Gabby did a little spin and asked, "Well, what do you think?"

"I think I'm overdressed," I said with a laugh.

She smiled. "What am I going to have to do to get you in a dress?"

"Get me in a gym so I can lose these thunder thighs."

We both laughed, but I was serious. Being a size sixteen wasn't a bad thing when you had been a size sixteen all your life. But I hadn't been. I went from being a size four to a size eight to a size twelve to a size sixteen, thanks to years of stress, bad eating, and having kids. My self-esteem was about as high as grass that had been freshly mowed.

"I don't know why you're so hard on yourself. The weight can be lost, but your self-esteem can't be bought. You have to cut that out. You look good, and you carry your weight well. It's not like you look like a popped can of biscuits."

We both had a good laugh at that one. It didn't take us long to get to the club. About twenty-five minutes with traffic. We paid to park, then walked the short distance to the place. The weather was a little hot and muggy, which attested to the rain the meteorologist had spoken about earlier. People were out in droves. Some headed to the club. Others headed to other places around. Good thing we'd decided to get there early. There was already a line at the door. That took us about another fifteen minutes.

"Twenty if you're just sitting at the bar. Ten if you're here to enjoy the band and dinner," the hostess told us once we got to the door.

Gabby went into her silver clutch and handed the woman a twenty; then we waited to be led to a table. The place may not have looked like much from the outside, but once on the inside, it was amazing. Red-stained concrete walls with black leather booths were on the side of the room with the stage. The other side had black walls with red circular tables and red and black chairs. A red carpet led from the door to the bar. Square, low-hanging light fixtures gave the room a dim lighting, along with the faux candles burning on the tables.

The place was already full, it seemed, but the line we had left outside told us it would be packed as the night progressed. Gabby and I did a little jig when we were led to a booth right in front of the stage.

"Thank you for joining us tonight at The Treble Cleft, ladies. We do hope your night is a memorable one. Your server will be with you shortly," the hostess told us.

We thanked her as she laid the food, dessert, and drink menus on our table. I didn't realize I was smiling until Gabby cast a sidelong glance at me.

"What?" I asked.

"Just happy to see you smiling is all."

"I figure I may as well try to find some kind of happiness while here."

She gave me a one-arm hug, then opened her menu. While we talked and joked the night away, I was feeling some type of way about the fact Malik hadn't tried to call me back. I checked my phone every so often, hoping for a text or something. Some kind of lifeline of hope.

"Want to tell me what's wrong?"

I turned to find Gabby eyeing me. I didn't even realize I had been staring off into space. The music was live. Both bands had shut the house down. While they had played, I'd been all into the moment. But when the music had stopped, my husband's voice was back. Even though I was all set to pretend everything was everything, Gabby's knowing eyes had locked in on me. So before I could lie like it was nothing, Gabby was shaking her head telling me not to even think about it. I chuckled a bit and sighed, then told her about Malik calling me earlier.

She was about to respond when the waiter came over to refill our wineglasses.

Once the waiter left, Gabby said to me, "Enjoy yourself this weekend. It's about you. Don't let any man take you away from remembering who you are. Don't ever lose yourself in a man. He will be okay, and if he isn't, then . . . oh well. He cheated on you, in your home. He should be begging on hands and knees."

I nodded because I knew she had a point, but what scared me most was that Malik wasn't groveling. He wasn't calling, texting, or trying to get me to forgive him. It was like he didn't even care. But, as she said, I had come to the island to enjoy myself. So I got back into the spirit of things and pushed Malik to the back of my mind. Everything was going well. Drinks were good, food was good, music was great . . . and then my wandering eyes started to roam the club.

I'd caught the eye of many of the men in the place who had been smiling at me and Gabby. I knew why they were looking at her. I figured the dimness of the club was blinding them to how I really looked. The all-black attire I had on hid the true thickness I possessed. Still, I just decided to look around to take my mind off of things . . . when I spotted him.

"Oh my damn," I said out loud before I could stop myself.

I picked up my wineglass and took a leisurely sip. Lord Jesus, that man's teeth were so damn white. His face held a goatee that was nice and even. His smooth, chocolate skin made me want to walk over and touch it. And he had locs. They sat braided back into six neat cornrows against his scalp. Anyone who knew me knew I was a sucker for men with long hair. Make that hair locs and I was smitten! He sat with a demeanor that read confident, not cocky. Eyes twinkled at me from behind his black-framed glasses. I guess the brother whose eyes I caught staring at me read my lips because he looked as if he chuckled, then nodded and smiled at me.

He was casually sitting on the red leather-top bar stool. One leg on the swivel and one leg on the floor. I could tell the loafers on his feet were expensive because of the red bottoms. He had on black dress slacks that strained against the muscles in his thighs. Big hands lured me in, one resting on his thigh while the other one held a glass with an amber-colored liquid. His black blazer was open and showed the red shirt underneath, top button open showing his solid chest peeking through.

He held my eyes for so long that something passed between us. I saw him studying me as if he wanted to get to know me in ways a man shouldn't want to know a married woman. I shivered. Felt as if I was being undressed, but it wasn't invasive enough to make me feel uncomfortable. I wondered if this was what Malik felt when he looked at Janay. I wondered if the man staring at me was married. Wondered if he had a wife somewhere who had no idea he was eye fucking me in a dimly lit jazz club.

Looking at the stranger with the liquid black eyes and alluring pull had brought wanton desires to the forefront of my mind. It didn't help that when I glanced behind him to the man he had been talking to that he too looked like he'd walked right out of African Heaven. He had a smooth, caramel skin tone that had been gently kissed by the sun. He stood regally and looked to be taller than most of the men in the room. He had a close-cropped haircut, razor tapered to perfection. The curly mane and light eyes showed his mixed heritage.

He stood in tan wide leg dress slacks that sat grown man low on his hips. Clearly, they had been tailored to fit his lean, sinewy body. His Polo-style shirt faded into the muscles in his upper body.

"Shell," Gabby called to me as she shook my shoulder.

"Oh. Huh?"

She shook her head. "I've been talking to you this whole time. What are you looking at? You okay?"

I looked at her. I hadn't even heard her calling me.

"I'm sorry, but look toward the bar," I told her. "Guy with the locs and his friend."

Gabby pretended to be picking up a cloth napkin from the table, then looked at the bar.

"Oh my," she exclaimed in a whisper.

"My sentiments exactly."

She sat back and took a sip of her drink, while I pretended the couples on the floor were of interest to me.

"They're coming over here," she told me.

My leg had started to shake under the table. My nerves were tap dancing all over the place, and the wedding ring on my finger started to burn.

"I know," I said.

I just didn't know what I was going to do next. I wasn't into the tit-for-tat thing. Didn't want to cheat on Malik because he had cheated on me. Didn't even know if I wanted to entertain another man, even in conversation. Still, Mr. Stranger was getting closer and closer to me, so I was going to have to say something to him whether or not I wanted to.

Chapter 4

Gabrielle

Beautiful weather, a gorgeous beach house, great food, and now this awesome jazz club; despite a rocky start, our weekend away was sizing up pretty nicely so far. I was glad Shell had agreed to go out tonight, because if anyone needed to get out of her own head, it was her. Thinking about it, if we had stayed in, we probably would have been sitting around commiserating about the respective losers in our lives, chomping on ice cream sundaes. Not that eating ice cream sundaes would have been a bad thing, but that only would have given Shell yet another reason to bring up Malik, the sordid cheating mess, and his incessant disapproval of everything she did.

For as long as I had known Shell, it appeared she could never do anything right in Malik's eyes. Mind you, I was an outsider looking in, but from my perch, I had a pretty good view of the situation. From the way she raised her children, to her cooking and cleaning skills, to the way she wore her hair, to the fact that she had put on weight— Shell could do nothing right. And yet, for someone whom he considered so flawed, it appeared to me that Malik was afraid to lose Shell to another man. Which is why I wasn't surprised when he went all Incredible Hulk on her, green with envy, when Shell started attending some of her classes on campus.

"Why the fuck you gotta go to the school? I thought all your classes were online," I once heard him say to her while we were on the phone. Shell's school offered the option of a complete online experience, on campus experience, or a combination of both, and although she explained to him that some of the classes were a bit more difficult for her to handle online, he didn't care. Her educational pursuits were not in the least bit important to him.

Malik especially felt threatened by Shell's Introduction to Criminal Law instructor, Professor Hall. He first saw the professor when Shell was taking his Legal Studies course via teleconference. Let's just say Malik knows Shell's type, and the professor fit that bill to a tee: tall, dark skinned, handsome, überfit, impeccably dressed, and nice long locs. Not to mention, he was intelligent, worldly, and was an overall great guy. Everything she could want in a man—and more. But to Shell, Professor Hall was just that, her professor, and she would never cross that line because she believed in the sanctity of marriage, and, unlike her wayward husband, took her vows seriously.

The professor had taken a liking to Shell because of her strong will, stellar work ethic, and determination. Taking her under his wing, he even went so far as to secure her an internship studying abroad in London, England, for a semester. Needless to say, that didn't go over well with Malik, and, much to her disappointment, she ended up turning down possibly the biggest opportunity of her life.

Although she didn't like sharing her personal business, Shell eventually told Professor Hall why she turned down the internship. Despite that, he still wouldn't give up on her; which was why he encouraged her to attend some of his classes on campus, in the hopes that she would reconsider the opportunity she was given, if not now, then sometime in the near future. He told her she had something special, and if she really wanted it badly enough, one day, she would a great attorney.

"Mischelle, you are one of my most promising students, and I don't want to see you waste all that potential. I respect your reasons for turning down the internship, but think about it this way; you're doing this not only for you, but for your children. This would be your legacy to them; an educated black woman who is able to stand on her own two feet. Just think about it, and when you're ready, I'll make it happen. I can promise you that."

Shell told me what he had said to her. She was in disbelief that someone, especially a man like Professor Hall, would go out of his way like that for her. In her mind, she didn't deserve it. Clearly, that line of thinking had Malik's negative influence all over it.

All of Malik's posturing was quite ironic, considering *he* was the one cheating for who knows how long. Then again, that could explain his attitude; he was stepping out on his marriage and was paranoid that Shell would do the same. As much as I didn't believe in cheating or getting revenge like that, it would definitely serve him right.

Although Malik did a number on Shell with his negative programming, I was pleased to see it wasn't working tonight. She looked absolutely fabulous. Apparently, I wasn't the only one who thought so. Several of the male patrons were giving her head nods and winks whenever she looked in their direction. And then there was the tall chocolate brotha heading our way. Shell had been eye hustling him for the better part of fifteen minutes or so. I should say they were eye hustling each other, because when I followed the direction of Shell's glance, I clearly saw him ogling her just as hard as she was ogling him.

As he approached our table, I could see how nervous Shell was. Her leg began to shake incessantly, and she started rocking like Miss Sophia from *The Color Purple*.

"Shell," I said, kicking her under the table, "what is the matter with you?"

"Are you seriously asking me that right now?" she replied, still rocking. "Look at him. And he's coming over here." My left hand was on the table. Shell grabbed it, squeezing the life out of it. "Gabby, he's coming over here!"

I pulled my hand back, trying to shake some circulation back into it. "No kidding, Shell. I can see you know. Now, stop the Miss Sophia routine and relax already."

"Okay." She stopped rocking, but then she started breathing like she was in a Lamaze class. I looked at her, shaking my head. Luckily, she stopped when the object of her distress reached our table.

"Good evening, ladies," he spoke, looking directly at Shell. "My friend and I saw you two lovely ladies sitting here alone and were wondering if we could join you. That is, if you're not waiting for anyone. Boyfriends? Husbands, perhaps?" The man had a baritone to his voice.

I glanced at Shell, pausing to see if she was going to respond. I could have sworn she was about to pass out from fright as she gazed up at the well-dressed stranger. For a moment, he looked very familiar to me, but for the life of me, I couldn't decipher why. Then it dawned on me . . . that picture of Professor Hall that Shell had shown me. Looking at this man, from the way he dressed to his neatly coiffed locs, there was clearly a striking resemblance. Yep, definitely her type.

Shell once told me that she used to be a huge flirt; could flirt as easily as she breathed. At the moment, I found that very hard to believe.

Her lack of a response was killing me, so I quickly chimed in. "No, we're not waiting for anyone. Just enjoying girls' night out. But please, join us." I motioned for the two men to sit.

Now, generally, I'm pretty paranoid. I guess that comes from being a New Yorker and from watching way too much *Investigation Discovery, Dead of Night, Fatal Encounters, Disappeared;* you name it, I've watched it. Not to mention, all too often I'd hear about some woman who was hurt or murdered by a man she had just met, so I was very leery of strangers. And sure, we didn't know them from Adam, but we were in a well-lit, very public place with loads of people around. What was the worst that could happen, right? However, that didn't stop me from moving Shell's and my drinks to the far side of the table, where only she and I could reach them. I'm just sayin'.

I got up to sit in the seat opposite Shell, allowing her dreamboat to sit next to her, while his friend took the spot next to me.

"My name is Carl," he said, extending his hand to Shell.

I was shocked when she actually reached out hers and shook it, although she still hadn't said a word.

"Hi, my name is Gabrielle. And my shy friend next to you is Shell."

"Nice to meet you, ladies. The ugly mug over there is Diego," Carl said, with a chuckle. We all laughed at that, even Shell.

Diego took my hand, placing a gentle kiss on the back of it. "Pleased to make your acquaintance," he said, his voice a deep bass with a hint of an accent.

"The pleasure's all mine," my lips replied faster my brain.

Did I just say that? Was I actually flirting with this man? Unlike Shell, I never did master the art of the flirt. It just wasn't my thing. I hadn't paid him much attention at first, as I was too busy trying to get Shell to talk, but looking at the man sitting beside me, I mean, *really* looking at him, I realized this man was . . . beautiful. I know it's strange hearing a man described in such a way, but it was true. He was drop-dead gorgeous.

A smooth complexion like a Werther's Original hard candy, light hazel eyes, dark curly hair, and a body that boldly proclaimed, "I spend a lot of time in the gym"; this man was definitely what Shell would call eye candy. Don't get me wrong. I've never been one to fall for the handsome face and nice body, but I could surely appreciate one when I saw it, and at the moment, Diego had my full appreciation.

"Not to pry, but what are you two stunning ladies doing here alone?" Diego asked. He was a slick-tongued charmer as well.

"Like I said, girls' night out. Actually, it's a girls' weekend. We both just needed to get away for some R&R," I responded, hoping I wasn't blushing.

Diego smiled, flashing his perfectly white teeth. "In that case, I hope we are not intruding."

I smiled back. "Not at all. We don't mind the company, do we, Shell?" I asked. She still appeared to be in a daze, so I once again kicked her under the table.

"Huh? Oh no, we don't mind," she finally answered.

"Ah, she speaks," Carl teased. "Does she dance as well?" He stood up, extending his hand to her.

"Sure she does," I interjected.

Yeah, I know I should have minded my own business, especially because Shell was a married woman, and according to her ratchet worse half, I was the whore of Babylon, but it was only a dance. Besides, from our vantage point, I had full view of the dance floor, so I would be keeping my eyes on both of them.

"You two go ahead, but stay where I can see you," I said, more serious than joking.

That got a response from Shell. "Yes, Mom. Whatever you say."

I was tempted to do something childish, like stick my tongue out at her, but I refrained. Instead, I gave her the "You better act like you know" look, then smiled at her. She smiled back, took Carl's hand, and allowed him to lead her to the dance floor.

Once they were gone, I shifted my focus back to the man sitting beside me. All of a sudden, I was at a loss for words, which, for me, was extremely rare. But then again, I was in a situation that I was not used to; talking one-on-one with a very attractive man. I had been in a relationship for twelve years, so I didn't have to worry about dating or having meaningful conversation. At that moment, it dawned on me . . . When it came to mackin', I had no skills whatsoever. It was a skill I never needed because every guy I dated was a friend first. I never had to worry about the awkward conversational pauses because we were already comfortable with each other.

Diego must have sensed my trepidation, because he broke the ice. "Gabrielle is a beautiful name. A beautiful name for a beautiful woman."

"Thank you," I replied, again hoping I wasn't blushing.

"Tell me, how does your boyfriend feel about you coming out here without him?"

Nice segue, I thought to myself. "I don't have a boy-friend."

"I'm guessing you don't have a husband either."

"Now why would you think that?" I questioned.

Diego pointed to my left hand. "Unlike your friend over there," he responded, nodding his head in Shell's direction, "you're not wearing a ring. Please correct me if I'm wrong."

I smiled at him, liking his candor. "Very observant," I uttered. "By the way, don't think I didn't notice the ring on Carl's finger," I countered, looking in Shell and Carl's direction. They appeared to be having a good time.

"But to answer your question, I am not, nor have I ever been, married. You?" I figured since he was all in my business, I was going to get into his.

Flashing me a grin, he answered, "I've never been married, and I don't have a girlfriend."

That was good to know, I thought.

"If you don't mind me asking, why are you single?"

I really didn't like talking about myself or my personal life, but there was something about Diego that I liked, and while I still intended to keep my guard up, there was no harm in letting him in on the bare minimum.

"I was in a very long relationship. I've been single for about six months. Honestly, I needed to get to know me again."

"That's understandable, although I would like to get to know you as well. That is, if you would allow me," he said, that megawatt smile lighting up his face.

I smiled back. "As entertaining as that might be," I started, "we're only here until Sunday, and there's a lot we want to do—"

"Such as?" he cut me off.

"Well, Shell and I planned to spend a good part of the weekend at the Savannah Black Heritage Festival. They have different events scheduled all weekend, and we already planned to check a few of them out."

He gave me a knowing look. "What a coincidence. Our company is sponsoring free health assessments at the fair. Blood pressure readings, HIV screenings, body composition, blood sugar testing, and cancer awareness. These are the issues affecting the black and Latino communities, so we wanted to focus on them at the fair. Our company is very big on community service," he said with pride.

Handsome, smart, and altruistic? Color me intrigued. I liked the direction the conversation was going in.

"You keep saying 'our company.' I'm assuming you mean yours and Carl's."

"Yes. Electron Enterprises. We specialize in computer chips."

He reached in his back pocket, pulling out his wallet, and fished out a business card, handing it to me. According to the card, Diego was the chief financial officer of the company; the moneyman. Impressive. Of course, anyone could hand you a business card nowadays and say they owned a company. Heck, I could create some great-looking business cards from Vistaprint, or on Microsoft Publisher, for that matter, and have people believing I owned a company too.

"Check out our website. Google us. We are actually a Fortune 500 company, and our employee satisfaction rating is one of the highest in the world," he boasted.

It appeared that he was once again reading my mind, because I fully intended to look them up the first chance I got.

"I'll do that," I said. "And I think I'll make it a point to stop by your booth too."

"I would be disappointed if you didn't," he said, flirtation in his tone. "But enough about me. Tell me more about you. What do you do?"

"Actually, I'm a doctor. I work in sports medicine."

Diego had a sly look on his face. "Beauty *and* brains. Nice."

"Thanks," I replied, feeling very self-conscious.

At that moment, I felt an awkward pause coming. Luckily, Shell and Carl returned to the table.

"Everything okay over here?" Carl asked, looking at Diego.

"We're doing just fine," Diego replied.

It could have been my imagination, but it seemed as if he was trying to give Carl the hint to get lost.

Before I could give any more credence to that thought, Shell broke in, "Carl, I have go to the ladies' room. Gabby, care to accompany me?"

While I was glad for the opportunity to get up and stretch my legs, I could tell by her tone of voice that Shell had something on her mind. "Sure. Diego, will you excuse me?"

He stood, and as he did, I realized how much he towered over me. Even in four-inch heels, he was more than a head taller than me. It was like he was the giant from Jack and the Beanstalk, and I was like, well . . . Jack.

He moved out of the way, allowing me to pass, but as he did, he leaned down, whispering in my ear, "Don't take too long."

I turned around, smiled at him, and said, "I won't." I think I put a little extra sway in my swagger as I walked to the ladies' room.

Once inside, I quickly spoke before Shell could utter a word. "Okay, what's wrong?"

"What makes you think something's wrong?" she asked, as she leaned against the solid black granite counter with a red marble sink.

Her eyes were cast downward looking at her shoes.

I leaned back against the black and red tiled wall, crossing my arms in front of me. "For one, I could hear it in your voice. Two, you can't even look me in the eyes. So, again, I ask you, what's wrong?"

Taking in a deep breath, then sighing, she replied, "Carl."

"Oh boy. What's wrong with him?" I questioned, raising an eyebrow and tilting my head to the side.

She began pacing back and forth in the large bathroom that was bigger than those at some airports. "Nothing. That's just it. We talked, we danced, and I enjoyed it. Really enjoyed it. Then I thought about Malik and our marriage. One very fucked-up marriage, but a marriage nonetheless."

As she walked back in my direction, I stopped her midpace, placing my hands on her shoulders. "Shell, look at me." She reluctantly complied. "The reason why we're here in the first place is to get your mind off of Malik and, as you so eloquently termed it, your effed-up marriage, so thinking about either of those subjects totally defeats the purpose. Besides, it was just conversation and dancing. I don't see the harm," I gently chided, removing my hands from her shoulders.

"But that's just it, Gabby. It didn't feel that way to me. Aside from Professor Hall, I haven't had that much fun talking to a man in a long time. He's intelligent, engaging, and actually asked me what I thought about things, like my opinion actually mattered."

"Unlike Malik," I quipped, causing her to roll her eyes at me. "I'm just saying. Am I wrong?"

"No, you're not. And that's why I started thinking about Malik."

"Well, that's a real buzz kill," I scowled. "Tell me, Shell, what exactly did you and Carl talk about? You two couldn't have been out there for more than, what, ten, maybe fifteen minutes?"

"I know it wasn't a long time, but we talked about a lot of things; school, politics, the law. Things I'm interested in. And it was like he was actually interested in what I had to say. He didn't make me feel stupid or insignificant."

Apparently this man was in the right place at the right time, just when Shell needed him to be. He gave her a much-needed boost in the self-confidence department. Unfortunately, that boost came from a man who had on a wedding ring. "I'm glad Carl made you feel good about yourself, but Shell, you do realize he's married, right?"

"Yes, he mentioned it briefly. From what I gathered, his wife is a piece of work, and the marriage is on the rocks."

"Hmph, I bet that's the same thing Malik told Janay." The look in Shell's eyes told me I may have pushed the envelope with that last comment. I didn't mean to be so brusque with her, but I needed her to understand that people can lie if it suited their purposes. "Sorry, I just don't want you to be taken in if Carl's not being honest with you. Who knows? He could be telling the truth, but even if he isn't, you shouldn't feel guilty about chatting with a man who can actually hold a conversation, and who actually listened to what you had to say. Okay, so you may be romanticizing things a bit, but so what? It's not like you're going to run off into the sunset with this man, right?"

"True, but I do feel a bit guilty. I'm enjoying spending time with a man who's not my husband. I should feel that way about being with my husband."

This time it was my turn to sigh. "And yet you don't, and we both know why. And I can guarantee you Malik is not feeling one sense of guilt over being with someone else. If he did, his lying, cheating, trifling, slimy behind would be back home with his wife and children. But, alas, he's not. You're not cheating, Shell, you're just letting off some tension in a harmless manner. As long as you don't cross the line, it's all good."

Deep down, she knew I was right. She huffed and replied, "I guess you're right. It's not like I'm gonna sleep with the guy or anything. We'll never see these guys again after we leave here anyway, so what's the harm?"

I fake coughed, pretending to clear my throat. "Welllllll, I'm not so sure about that last part," I said.

"Why not?" Now, Shell was the one to cross her arms in front of her.

"Diego and Carl have a booth at the fair, so there is a chance we may run into them."

"What kind of booth?"

"Doing health assessments. They own a company, and, according to Diego, they are very much into community service."

"Company? Carl never mentioned anything about a company."

"Maybe he doesn't like talking about himself. You know I don't like talking about myself. Regardless of his reasons for not saying anything, Diego did give me his card." I handed it to Shell. "He said to check them out." We looked at each other, pulling out our cell phones at the same time. "I'll check the company Web site. You Google the company."

Shell and I discovered that Diego and Carl did indeed own Electron Enterprises. We also found out that it was one of the fastest-rising companies in the country, boasting over 25 million dollars in profits within two years, well on their way to making billions in profits within the next five. That was impressive for a relatively new company. And Diego was also telling the truth when he said the company had a strong focus on community service.

Not only did they sponsor health fairs, but food and clothing drives, literacy campaigns, and a whole host of other community service projects. They also had an on-site employee health facility, as well as a day care for the children of employees. Shell found links to articles where they were profiled in both *Black Enterprise* and *Forbes* magazine. Now I was *really* impressed. Not by the fact that Diego had money, because men with money never impressed me, but by the fact of how he got his money, and that he gave back. I found that very attractive.

"Looks like we all have something to talk about when we get back out there," Shell said, a slight smile on her face. "But before we do, tell me, what happened with you and Diego?"

"Nothing happened with me and Diego. We talked the entire time."

Glaring at me, she said, "Gabby, you're going to tell me you two only talked business?"

"Now I didn't say that." I flashed her a slick smile. "We talked about other things too."

"Like?"

"The fact that we're both unattached for starters."

"Really? And who started that conversation?"

And she accused *me* of sounding like someone's mother.

"He did. And before you go any further, just because we're both single doesn't mean I'm ready for any kind of relationship."

"Who said anything about a relationship?" Shell teased. I was glad she was able to find some levity, despite what was going on with her. "I'm just saying if the opportunity to have a little fun presents itself, just roll with it. After all, unlike me, you are single. And if anyone deserves a bit of gratuitous fun, it's you, my friend."

"Shell, you know darn well I'm not the 'roll with it' type." I made air quotes with my fingers.

"Well, maybe for once you should be." There was a seriousness to her tone.

"Anyway, I think we've kept them waiting long enough. Shall we?" I held the door open.

As we exited, Shell replied, "All I'm saying is, never say never. The night is still young."

I remembered one particular line that the hostess said to Shell and me earlier in the evening: "We do hope your night is a memorable one." Shell was right; the night was still young . . .

Chapter 5

Mischelle

Michael Buble's rendition of "Sway with Me" livened the place up as the singers took a break. The jazz band was all into the jubilant mood of the patrons. They were all smiles as they made love to their instruments and looked out onto the dance floor. The way Carl had been holding me as we moved in sync should have made me run for the hills. Not to mention, for a man of his stature, he was light on his feet and guided my movements as any good dance partner should.

As a married woman, no other man should have been sending jolts of electricity up my spine the way Carl had done. But it had been too long since I'd felt that all-knowing spark, that spark of sexual desire. The heat between a man and woman that left no doubt the sexual tension was thick. I couldn't explain why when Carl looked at me, everything that made me a woman came to life. The look he gave me reminded me that I still had life inside.

He didn't see me just as a mother and a wife. He'd held me like I was a woman, *his* woman. Which was odd since he was married too. I hadn't felt like a woman in a while. I felt like I was just going through life. I was mommy, wife, student. There was no particular order to it either.

"Were you telling me the truth about what's going on with you and your wife?" I'd asked Carl as we swayed on the dance floor.

With one hand on my waist and the other on the small of my back, he gazed down at me. "Why do you ask?" he replied.

The smirk on his face and humor in his eyes alarmed me if for no other reason than I knew what he was thinking. No man looked at a woman the way he was looking at me unless he had every intention of sampling what she had to offer. Even though I was quite tipsy, I still had my senses about me. There would be no sampling of anything I had. Especially not when both of us were married. For some reason, no matter what Malik had done, I couldn't bring myself to do unto him as he had done unto me.

"Your wife wouldn't have a problem with you eye hustling me? Dancing with me like this?" I asked.

"I really don't think she would care one way or the other."

His answer made me imagine the conversations Malik had with his whore. "What kind of wife do you have?"

"The kind who only cares about what she wants."

In that brief moment, I saw a flicker of darkness cloud his eyes. Then, just as quickly, it was gone. If I was to be honest, I could admit that his wife sounded a lot like my husband. So, I knew that look in his eyes. Still, I would never be the woman to speak badly about her husband to another man, especially one I didn't know. I should have realized the cheese was rotten in Denmark in that moment. Maybe it was because of the woodsy, spicy smell of the cologne he had on that I overlooked those signs. The scent carried an herbaceous top note reminiscent of fresh frankincense. I felt as if I was being hypnotized.

Gazing up into his eyes while he smiled and talked had the potential to be my undoing. I should have been ashamed of myself acting like a high school girl in heat instead of a mature, married mother of two. I couldn't help myself though. All I could think about was how sexy Carl was in every aspect. He was a gentleman through and through. Someone had taught him the importance of making a woman feel she was worthy of chivalry. Not to mention, he was a great distraction to take my mind off Malik.

"You having a good time so far?" Diego asked once Carl and I walked back over to the table.

I noted the light accent—Spanish, if I had to guess— in his voice. The smile he carried was a mesmerizing one, and I could tell those two together were lady killers.

"So far, so good," I answered.

The four of us discussed how well the club was set up and the great talent of the band. Diego and Carl ordered another bottle of wine. I knew I shouldn't have had anything else to drink, but when Carl placed another glass into my hand, I eagerly took it. While Carl bobbed his head to the music, I tried not to pay attention to the way his muscled thighs rubbed against my mine each time he would tap his feet to the beat. I ignored the strong chiseled chin. Shook my head at how smooth his chocolate skin was. Couldn't help the fact I wanted to run my hand through his locs and see what they would look like hanging and swaying around his shoulders.

Once again, my mind shifted back to Malik. I slyly checked my phone to see if he had tried to call me again. Nothing. It was clear that he just didn't give a fuck. It had me trying to figure out at what point I had lost my husband.

I tried to get back to the moment at hand. The conversation was going well. Carl was even comfortable enough to pick up one of the extra forks on the table and taste the crab cake that I hadn't eaten. We ended up sharing while Diego tried to figure out why Gabby wasn't interesting in dating.

"You both live in ATL?" Diego wanted to know.

Gabby shook her head. "I live in North Carolina."

"Oh, I see," he responded.

"You're originally from Atlanta?" Carl asked me.

I shook my head. "No. I grew up in Mississippi until I was about thirteen. Then my mother met my stepfather, and he moved us to Atlanta."

He chuckled. "What a coincidence. My mother is from Mississippi."

"Yeah? What part?"

"Yazoo County."

"Wow, that's pretty close to me in Holmes County."

"I'll take that as saying we were meant to meet eventually."

"Because your mother and I are from the same state?" I asked with a laugh.

He nodded as he wiped his mouth with a red cloth napkin. "That, and the fact that you felt me watching you."

I couldn't lie. There had been something in the air that pulled my attention toward the bar. There was that feeling you get when you either felt somebody was following you or someone was watching you. I'd felt that energy strongly.

I took a sip of my wine, glanced out onto the dance floor, then back to Carl. "How do you know that?"

"I felt it when you looked at me. And when you didn't immediately break eye contact, I knew you could feel what I was feeling."

"I don't know what feeling you're talking about," I lied.

He knew I was lying, but being the gentleman he was, he wouldn't call me on it. I'd actually been feeling him since the moment I laid eyes on him, but there would be no way I'd tell him that. I didn't hide the fact that the ring on his finger had my attention though.

He saw me looking. Made a show of removing his ring and dropping it in his shirt pocket. Then he picked up his drink, Crown Royal on ice, and took a sip.

"Doesn't mean shit to me if it doesn't mean shit to you," he said nonchalantly.

I shook my head in disbelief, then found myself getting angry. Is this what married men did when they met new women? Act like the vows they took meant nothing?

I told him, "I'm not taking my ring off."

"You don't have to. I took mine off to make you comfortable."

"It wasn't bothering me."

He gave a lopsided grin. "That's good to know."

Even before finding out Malik had cheated on me, he and I hadn't had sex in a while. Probably more so my fault than his at this point. But that was only because Malik had forgone the foreplay part of sex. His idea of asking me for sex was asking me to "handle his dick."

As the night progressed, Carl and I kept the conversation light. The flirting crept in occasionally. The alcohol was getting to me. My breasts had swelled, nipples hardened, and my lotus had definitely bloomed. I crossed my legs to stave off the crippling feel of needing to release. I hadn't had an orgasm in over a year. Carl moved closer to me once the group started singing again. His eyes never left mine as the pad of his thumb traced my lips. I could feel every pressure point I had burst alive. His touch made me feel like I was the only woman in the world and the only one who mattered.

I remembered a time when Malik had made me feel that way. Remembered when he would take his time to kiss me like he didn't want to forget my taste. Over the past year, his idea of foreplay had been a quick lick on my pussy and a tap against my clitoris. I missed the days when Malik used to take his time with my body. He used to lick me from the front to the back. There hadn't been a place on my body that Malik's tongue hadn't been. Hell, his favorite pastime used to be tossing my salad. These days we barely kissed.

I couldn't get past the nicotine and the smell of smoke to kiss him like I wanted to, and he didn't seem to care whether I kissed him or not. And now I knew why . . .

Kissing.

Damn, it had been a long time since I had been kissed so thoroughly. Malik hadn't taken the time to let his tongue trace the outline of my lips before nibbling on the bottom one, then sucking it into his mouth. He placed one hand on my waist to ease me closer to him while the other one gently caressed my face as our tongues danced the night away.

Nah, Malik didn't let his tongue hit the roof of my mouth and send chills back down my spine. Malik's kisses had been a question mark, while Carl's kiss was the exclamation point to my arousal.

Oh shit, my mind cried. *Shell, you're kissing another man, and he's not your husband. You're kissing another woman's husband,* my mind screamed, but for the life of me, I wouldn't be able to stop if I wanted to. Carl's kiss was slow, steady, and deliberate. It was clear he was set on sampling me one way or the other.

His kiss had been a prelude to passion, a rapport enacted physically with the promise of something more erotic to come. I was in trouble. The thrill of experiencing something I hadn't in over a year, a mind-numbing orgasm, and something I'd never experience . . . a man with length and girth. I'd already started praying to the sex gods that Carl knew what to do with all he was packing. I was so heated, my nipples had started to push through the fabric of my bra causing a slight tingle of pain that stimulated me more.

When Carl's hand moved down my waist to roam over the curves of my hips, I didn't stop him. That same hand gripped my thigh and when he moaned into my mouth, I was pretty much his to do with what he wanted. *Damn, bitch, you're easy,* my conscious screamed. *You're a whore just like the woman screwing your husband,* my mind yelled once more.

I tensed when Carl's hand gripped the back of my braids. Something about that aggressive move made me feel more alive. I got brazen in my dance with the devil. Allowed my hands to travel up his thighs. One hand fondled the length I felt behind his zipper, and the other mapped the muscles in his chest. I could feel what made him a man anatomically swell so regally under my intense scrutiny.

Carl pulled back from the kiss, growled low as he looked into my eyes, then said to me, "He doesn't matter to me, if she doesn't matter to you."

I knew what he was asking. Knew what he wanted. I held the answer to his question.

Chapter 6

Gabrielle

My mouth dropped open. I couldn't believe what I was seeing. If I could, I would have taken out my contact lenses and put them back in, just to make sure my eyes weren't playing tricks on me. Shell and Carl were sitting directly in front of Diego and me, swapping spit and playing tonsil hockey like they were the only two people in existence. I might actually be happy for Shell if it wasn't for the fact that they were both married.

What in the heck was she thinking? I mean, I knew she was somewhat under the influence, but I think it was less about the alcohol and more about her need to feel something—anything. As much as I couldn't stand Malik and everything he had done, she *was* married to him, albeit unhappily. And yet, here she was, breaking her marriage vows for all the world to see.

Clearly, I wasn't the only one who thought they were making a spectacle of themselves. Diego looked shell-shocked, and some of the other patrons were staring as well. For the second time tonight, I kicked Shell under the table. She gazed in my direction, shooting me the most venomous look I had ever seen. Oh yes, Shell was ticked, but I'd rather have her angry with me now than for her to do something she would regret later.

As far as I knew, she had never broken her vows, not a single solitary one, and despite her husband being a gaping lying, cheating butthole, I knew she still loved him. Yeah, she looked, but she had never, *ever* touched, never stepped outside of her marriage. Which was why, for the life of me, I couldn't figure out why Shell was acting like a single woman on the prowl. Or like she belonged to another man. This simply was not like her. But then again, when a man has constantly beat you down emotionally and mentally on a daily basis, I could actually understand her urge to act so impulsively.

I mean, here was an extremely attractive man showing her the attention she yearned for, attention that she should have been getting from her husband, but wasn't. In a few short minutes, Carl had given Shell something that she hadn't received in months: an awareness that she was desired and wanted. I could appreciate that feeling. I'd been there myself, and could easily sympathize with her situation.

Just as I was contemplating having another discussion with Shell, I felt my purse vibrate. I hadn't checked my cell all evening, mainly because there was no reason for anyone to call me while I was away, unless it was extremely important. I took the phone out of my purse just in case it was something urgent. When I looked at the screen, I saw who the call was from; it was Daniel. He was probably still salty about this morning, but that was *his* problem, not mine. I promptly pressed the ignore button on the screen.

Noticing I had some text messages, I entered my pin number, then looked to see who they were from. I rolled my eyes, seeing they were all from Daniel. Thanks for leaving me hanging . . . Where are you? . . . Oh, so now you're ignoring me? The messages went on and on. I guess he got tired of texting and decided to call instead. Not five minutes later, he called back, and once again, I ignored him. I really should have turned my phone off, but I always kept it on in case of an emergency. When he called for the third time, I decided to answer, intent on nipping him in the bud once and for all. I excused myself from the table, heading outside.

"Yes, Daniel," I answered, trying to sound less annoyed than I actually was.

"Why didn't you answer me before?" he asked.

"Because I'm on vacation, remember? I'm trying to enjoy myself."

"Oh, and you don't have two seconds to answer my call?"

"Is it something important?"

"Well, unless you don't consider me losing my job as important, then I guess not. You just bounced like you didn't even care."

I took in a deep breath, taking a *woosah* moment before answering him. "Daniel, I took you in after you showed up at some unholy hour in the middle of the night pissy drunk, interrupting what little sleep I was trying to get, mind you. Now, I didn't have to do that, but out of concern for you, and because I didn't want you driving like that, I let you stay. I tried to talk to you, but you passed out before I even had a chance. Now I feel bad about you losing your job, but there was nothing I could do for you. This trip was planned a long time ago, and I wasn't going to miss it."

"Oh, so you're telling me that gallivanting around like you're twenty-one with someone who should be at home with her kids is more important than me?"

In no time flat I went from annoyed to flat-out fuming. I was trying to be compassionate because of his situation, but Daniel was not making it very easy.

"Hey, things look bad right now, but you'll find something. I'm sure of it. In the meantime, if you need a few dollars to get by, then I'll help you out. But it will have to wait until I get back." As the words left my mouth, I had a bad feeling that my promise to help him would come back to bite me in the butt later on.

"I appreciate that, but I want to talk to you now. Are you really that busy?"

I couldn't win for losing. I moved the phone away from my ear, looking at it with a confused expression as if Daniel was directly in front of me.

"Look," I said, all calmness gone out of my voice, "I can't talk right now. I'm out, and I'm being rude by standing out here talking to you. If I can, I will call you later."

"You know what—fuck it!" he yelled. "Go on, hang out with your little girlfriend. I'll deal on my own."

Next thing I heard was a click on the other end of the phone. So much for trying to relax. I was so heated I had half a mind to call him back. I was about to when I felt the presence of someone behind me. I turned to see Diego looking down at me.

"How long have you been standing there?" I asked.

"Not long. I wanted to see if you were okay. You were gone for a while."

"I'm fine. Nothing serious."

I hadn't noticed it at the time, but the temperature had dropped quite a few degrees, and while it was still unseasonably warm, the night air had taken on a bit of a chill.

"Are you sure? You seem upset." He appeared genuinely concerned.

I put on my best poker face and replied, "Yes, I'm sure. It's nothing I can't handle."

"If you say so." He looked skeptical. "You're shivering," Diego said.

I should have brought a jacket with me, but I was so excited about Shell and me going out, the thought had completely slipped my mind. "A little, but I'll be okay."

Walking past me, Diego deactivated the alarm to a graphite luster metallic Acura MDX. He had conveniently gotten a valet parking space directly in front of the club. Opening the side door, he took a black leather jacket off one of the seats and placed it around my slender shoulders. It felt heavy, but it did take the chill off. Then he climbed into one of the vehicle's middle seats, motioning for me to join him. I gave him a look that said, "I don't know you like that."

Catching the hint, he flashed that sexy smile of his, saying, "I'll leave the door open. And you can even have the keys." He held them up for me to see.

I cautiously approached the car, climbing in with my hand outstretched. I took the keys from him, then sat in the seat next to him.

"You must be from New York," he laughed.

"Why do you say that?" I asked, furrowing my brow.

"Because you're paranoid just like one," he teased.

I laughed. "Oh, is that right? Hey, a girl has to protect herself, you know."

"I completely agree," he said, putting up his hands as if in surrender. "If I had a sister, I would want her to be just as careful. It's just New York knows New York."

I knew there was a reason I liked him, besides the obvious.

"Really, now? Do tell," I said as I leaned back in the seat, making myself comfortable.

"I'm originally from the Bronx. Southside. Now I live in downtown Brooklyn."

"*I'm* from Brooklyn," I said, pride in my voice.

"Why did you leave New York?"

"The weather," I remarked.

"So you wimped out, huh?" he quipped, with a wink.

"Whatever," I said, snickering.

I grew up in the Flatbush section of Brooklyn, a place I termed "The Little West Indies" because of the diverse people that lived there: Barbadians, Jamaicans, Trinidadians, Haitians, Puerto Ricans, Dominicans, and, of course, black Americans. A few white people, Asians, and Indians lived in the neighborhood as well. I was usually good at placing accents, but Diego's confused me a bit.

"Where are your parents from, because, for the life of me, I cannot figure out your accent."

He smiled. "My father is Afro-Cuban, and my mother is Puerto Rican. I spent a lot of time in both places growing up."

"That explains it. I like your accent though."

"I like yours too."

I gave him a quizzical look. "Diego, I don't have an accent."

"I know," he kidded.

I shook my head.

Diego and I talked on and on and discovered we both liked sports. You couldn't be a true New Yorker without liking some type of sport. For baseball, we both like the New York Mets; football, the New York Giants; and for hockey, I liked the New York Rangers, while he liked the New Jersey Devils. Diego was a tried-and-true New York Knicks fan. Since the New Jersey Nets became the Brooklyn Nets, my loyalty was split between the two teams.

The conversation had been so good that neither one of us realized that we had been outside talking for a good forty-five minutes until I checked the time on my phone.

"Wow, we've been gone for a long time. You think Shell and Carl are okay in there?"

"I think they are doing just fine without us around," Diego remarked. "Honestly, I came outside to check on you, but I also felt like a third wheel in there."

I already knew Shell's motivation for her actions, but I had no idea what drove Carl to do what he did. I figured who better to ask for some insight than his good friend.

"Diego, I'm curious. Why did Carl push up on Shell? I mean, with him being married and all."

"Why did Shell allow him to push up on her? She's married too," he countered.

"Touché. It's just, I know why Shell is acting the way she is, and I don't want her to get caught up in something that she may not be able to get out of."

"It appears both our friends have their reasons for their actions. All I will say is they're two consenting adults. Whatever happens, they will have to deal with it. Right now, I'm more concerned with the woman sitting next to me. I feel like dancing. Think you can keep up?" he asked with a sly grin.

It had been so long since I had danced with someone. I hoped that I hadn't forgotten how, but he didn't need to know that. "Can you?" I shot back, smiling.

"We'll see," he replied, as we started to exit the car.

I attempted to take off Diego's jacket, but he stopped me. "Hold on to it," he said. "You may need it later."

I smiled at his chivalry. After I stepped out of the car, I handed the keys back to him, allowing him to lock up and reset the alarm. As we walked the few steps back to the club and he opened the door for me, I thought about how the night had already taken several unexpected twists and turns. I had to wonder how many more would come before our night was over.

Chapter 7

Diego

My cell rang out in the middle of the night, waking me from a long-needed sleep. I ignored it. Sent whoever was on the other end to voice mail so my restful peace wouldn't be disturbed. I'd just turned over and gotten settled into another comfortable position when my house phone blared alive like it was a siren, a warning bell. I groaned loudly, turned over, and grabbed the cordless contraption from its cradle. I didn't bother to look at the caller ID. Whoever it was had better be in a life-or-death situation.

"What?" I solemnly answered.

"Diego," the female's voice on the other end called out to me.

I turned onto my back and let out a sigh as I rubbed my eyes.

"Yeah," I responded.

Something crashed in her background, like a loud explosion, while she screamed.

"Please come and get Carl. I don't want to call the police, but I'm scared. He's scaring me, and I don't know who else to call," she said frantically.

I glanced over at the woman in my bed, wondering why in the hell I'd allowed her to stay past the moment of sex. Throwing my legs over the side of the bed, I stood, anxiety riding me like waves beating against the shore.

That loud crashing explosion sounded in the woman's background again.

"What's going on, Dalisay?" I asked her.

"Carl, stop!" she yelled at him before answering me, frantically. "He just snapped. Went crazy—"

"Open the fucking door," I heard Carl's booming voice in the background. "Bitch, I ought to kill your mother-fucking ass," I heard.

That woke me up. Something had gone wrong in fairy tale land. Carl and Dalisay had the perfect marriage . . . or so it had seemed. They'd gotten married a few years after college and things had been perfect for them ever since. Dalisay was a rising partner in her corporate law firm. Carl and I were two of the top dogs in the microchip business.

I knew Carl loved and respected his wife, so the fact that she had locked herself in a room and he was threatening physical harm alarmed me. Something major had to have happened.

I flipped the light on in my bedroom. Saw the mess Ricki and I had made when we decided on a nightcap back at my place. My stained hardwood floor had her black thong, jeans, shirt, and shoes strewn about, right along with my suit from the workday. Ricki's rounded chocolate backside was a greeting even God could appreciate. She lay on her stomach, shapely legs positioned in the number four while she softly slept in the California king-size bed.

Her wild 'fro covered the side of her face. Scratches adorned her hips and thighs from where my nails had grazed her as she tried to ride me without falling off. She'd lost that fight. Golden condom wrappers littered the floor by the bed, and the sweet smell of our sex permeated the air. As much as I would have liked to slip back between those shapely thighs, she had to go. She didn't have to go home, but she had to get the hell up out of my place.

As rude as it may have sounded, Ricki understood. She and I had been doing that same song and dance for the better part of three years. I tapped her backside to wake her up. Waited until she got her bearings about her. She awakened, then looked around for a few minutes while her eyes and mind adjusted.

"I have to go?" she asked once lucid.

I nodded as I tossed her clothing to her. She smacked her lips and gave a sigh, but rose without a fight.

"Dali, what in hell is going on over there?" I asked, bringing my attention back to the woman on the other end of my phone.

"Oh, God, Diego, just please hurry up and get here. I don't want my husband to go to jail. I'm trying not to call the cops, but he's scaring me, and one of my neighbors may call the police," she pleaded. "Just get him to calm down for me please."

"Calm down for what? Tell me what's going on."

I rushed around the room grabbing up my discarded clothing. Thought about actually finding something else to wear altogether, but the direness of the situation didn't give me time. I grabbed my boxer briefs, white sleeveless ribbed cotton tee shirt, and gray suit slacks. Ricki sauntered into the bathroom like she was floating. I gave her a smack on her backside and tapped my watch to get her moving. She jumped, cut her eyes at me, but got my message.

"Just get here, Diego. Please."

I hung up the phone, tossed it on the bed, then quickly threw my clothes on. I prayed traffic would be nice to me. Coming from downtown Brooklyn heading to Garden City, Long Island would be damn near an hour's drive, depending on traffic. So I silently prayed that whatever was going on between the two didn't escalate before I could get there.

I grabbed my cell and my car keys and waited for Ricki to slide her feet into the brown wedge pumps. She scurried past me, bra and underwear still in her hand. I watched her backside as her hips called to me. Ricki walked like her entire existence was to hypnotize a man with the sway of her hips. I'd always been a sucker for darker skinned women. The darker she was, the better. Ricki ran a hand through her 'fro as we walked across the glass floor, then descended down the spiraled staircase with stainless steel railing.

"Are we still on for tomorrow?" she asked me once we got into the hall.

I had promised to take her to a show on Broadway. Told her to pick what she wanted and we would go. That was the way it was between us. It was rare I told her no because it was even rarer that she gave me a hard time.

"I don't know yet. Let me see what's going on with Carl first."

She knew who Carl was. She'd been around long enough to know quite a few of my friends and associates.

"Okay. Well, I guess I'll see you whenever you have time."

"I'll call you to let you know what's up."

She nodded. Stood on her toes to kiss my lips once the doorman opened the door for us to walk outside. Her lips were full, soft, and plush. I placed my hand on the small of her back as I returned the kiss. She smiled as we both pulled away. I didn't know why she hadn't worn her coat outside. The chill in the air was almost crippling. Yet, all she had on was a thin blouse. I took my jacket off and handed it to her. Walked her to her car and waited for her to get in before taking my jacket back.

One of the reasons Ricki was still around was because she followed the rules when it came to being with me. I wasn't looking for love. Didn't need the headache of having to account for my time and actions. I simply wanted a friend with benefits. Someone I could call and chill with from time to time. Someone I could take out on the town, catch a few shows on Broadway, dinner a few times, and some good sex. Once I was ready for the night to end, I needed a woman who didn't have a problem with me asking her to leave. Better yet, I needed one who I didn't have to tell to leave. Ricki was good with all of that. And that was why she was still around.

Yeah, I kept money in her pocket. Made sure she got an allowance every month. What man would have sexual relations with a woman, and then be reluctant to help her when she needed him to? I wasn't that kind of man. While Ricki never asked for anything unless she needed it, which was hardly ever, I still had her bank account number. I kept her pockets filled so when the time came, she wouldn't have a problem keeping me satisfied. What we had worked.

Yes, at forty, I still wasn't in a hurry to settle down or start a family. I didn't get that nagging incessant urge to find a woman to settle down with. At least that was the lie I told myself.

I was thankful traffic wasn't bad. Sometimes at two thirty in the morning, traffic in Brooklyn could still be a curse. I made it to Garden City in a little under an hour. I pulled into the long driveway. The tan and golden brick structure looked menacing in the dark. Like the outside told of the anger inside. The black-framed windows and mahogany doors seemed to be scowling under the strain.

I parked my car in front of the garage, behind Carl's black-on-black Mercedes. I could see a few neighbors had their lights on. Some had even come outside, not caring to hide the fact they were trying to see what was going on. The last thing I wanted to have happen was a scared, timid, white woman calling the police on an angry black man.

I would have knocked on the door, but since it was already cracked open, there was no need. The foyer looked as if a hurricane had torn through it. Pictures had crashed on the floor like they had been thrown against the wall. Several holes were in the walls, like Carl had taken his anger out on them since he couldn't hit his wife. Papers lay strewn about in disarray. Dali's clothes and shoes had been tossed over the railing like they were yesterday's trash. Makeup, makeup brushes, and the like painted the foyer's marble flooring.

"Seventeen years," I heard Carl roar out. "Seventeen fucking years of marriage and for what? So you could go and screw around on me?"

The front room had furniture overturned. Bookshelves had been knocked down. But my ears perked up when I heard his accusation. That would explain why Carl had been acting strange as of late. He'd always been a hard worker, but for him to be in our office in Manhattan before me meant he had to be sleeping in his hideaway office at work. Since the day we had formed the business together, Carl had never clocked in before I did. I'd asked him about it, but he just brushed me off, saying he wanted to make sure the new project stayed ahead of task. I didn't question him about it because I too had wanted to stay ahead of task.

I rushed up the grand staircase two steps at a time when I heard Dalisay screaming again.

"Carl, please, stop. I'm sorry," she sobbed.

I followed their voices until I got to one of their guest bedrooms. There, I found Carl trying to put his foot through the bathroom door. *The room had been turned upside down just like the rest of the house. The bed had been flipped. Dressers had been turned over. Carl's ropey locs swung angrily, back and forth, when he placed his booted foot against the white door. If the door hadn't been thick, he would have surely kicked it down. He was dressed in black sweats and a black tee shirt, his muscles bulging anytime he inhaled and exhaled.*

"I know you're sorry, you fucking bitch. You fuck another man in my house, in my bed!"

Say what? *I thought as I rushed into the room.*

"Yo, Carl, what in hell is going on?" *I asked him.*

He didn't even spare me a look, just kept trying to kick the door down.

"Carl," *I called to him again, this time with much more bass in my voice.* "You have to chill. Your neighbors are going to call the cops."

"Tell them to call. The only way I don't put my foot in this bitch's ass is if they kill me first."

There wasn't any doubt in my mind he meant every word coming out of his mouth. I'd never heard Carl refer to Dalisay with such disdain. I didn't have time to think about that though. My sole purpose for the moment was to keep him out of jail. I walked over to the man I'd called a good friend for over twenty years and shoved him backward. For the first time, I got a good look at the madness behind his eyes. They seemed glossed over, as if rage had taken away his common sense. The black-framed glasses he had on did nothing to take away from his imposing presence.

"What you need to do," *I told him,* "is calm the hell down before you do something you can't take back. I get that you're angry, but you still need to think before you act, my man."

"That's a coldhearted bitch hiding in the bathroom," he snarled.

When his big hands balled into a fist and I saw a tear escape the corner of his right eye, I knew what Dali had done to Carl had broken him down to his core.

"Seventeen fucking years I've been faithful," he fumed, then bit down on his bottom lip. "I've done everything she asked of me, and then some. Went above and beyond to be what she wanted and needed. All for this bitch to fuck another nigga raw and be carrying his seed."

My eyes widened, and I tilted my head to the side. "Say what now?"

I listened while Carl ranted and raved. I had a good mind to move to the side and help him kick the door down. Was he honestly telling me that Dalisay had cheated on him and was pregnant with another man's baby?

I could hear her sobbing loudly in the bathroom. "I didn't mean for this to happen, I swear."

"Oh, what, so you just ended up on his dick by accident?" Carl boomed.

"I swear it just happened. I didn't mean for things to go this far. John and I . . . we—I made a mistake, Carl."

"You don't make a mistake and fuck another nigga raw, Dali," he belted out as his left fist slammed into the open palm of his right one. "You don't make those kinds of mistakes. Then you let him come into our home, the fucking home I helped you to build, and you fuck this nigga in our home. That ain't no fucking mistake!"

Dali slowly pulled the door open. Her sun-kissed skin was flushed with tears, giving her a ruddy undertone. Silky brown hair cascaded down her shoulders while her light brown eyes held the fear she had of her husband, a man who'd never lifted a hand to her other than to help. I saw the bruises on her arms and wrists. I shook my head. Carl had lost his mind. I couldn't help *that my eyes traveled to her stomach. She didn't look pregnant.*

She slapped her tears away as she looked at me, then dropped her head. I guess the shame was too heavy to hold. Dali was beautiful in her own right. She was Filipino and proud of her race and heritage. She was what black men considered exotic, the kind we went crazy over and oftentimes preferred over our own race of women. Not that I had anything against interracial dating, I just didn't appreciate the notion that any other race of woman was better than my own simply because the other woman was of another race.

Dali tried to move toward Carl, and he bristled, frowned his face at her like she was a random whore on the street. He made a move toward her, and I blocked his path.

"Mrs. Robinson," I heard someone call from downstairs. "Mrs. Robinson, it's Officer Davis, your neighbor. My wife wanted me to check on you. Are you okay?"

Dali quickly wiped her eyes and rushed to the hall. I heard her assuring the officer that she was okay as she descended the stairs. Officer Davis asked about the bruises on her arms and wrist. Asked if her husband was home. She answered yes.

"Who did this?" he asked her.

I told Carl, "You need to pack a bag. You can't stay here tonight."

"I ain't packing shit," he snapped. "She's leaving. I'm not. I didn't desecrate my home with some random pussy. I married a whore, a fucking whore."

"Carl, I know you're pissed, but if that white woman has sent her husband over here, your black ass is only one step away from jail."

Carl snarled at me. "This is my fucking house, and I'm. Not. Leaving," he bellowed out, enunciating each syllable in the last three words spoken.

His pride was talking, had a hold on his ability to make intelligent decisions. Carl's jaw was clenched. Veins popped out on the sides of his head. When I heard the officer yell for Carl to come downstairs, I knew shit was going from bad to worse. I knew the only thing that would get Carl to calm down at that point was for Dali to leave, and since she refused to, once Officer Davis called in for backup, they'd make Carl leave. He could either leave or be arrested for domestic violence.

"Let's just leave," I told him. "At least leave for the night and calm down. Come back when you're thinking rationally. You don't want to be arrested right now. Actually, our business can't afford for you to get arrested. All the meetings and shit we got scheduled for this deal with Apple and Microsoft won't allow it. So grab a bag and chill at my place for the time being," I reasoned with him.

After a few more not-so-pleasant words to Dali and another threat of detainment, Carl took my advice. I waited around anxiously as he packed a bag and answered a few questions for the police. I only knew parts of what they knew. So there wasn't much for me to tell them.

It was only because Officer Davis knew Carl and Dali that he didn't take Carl to jail. Although Carl left, he didn't come back to my place. He told me he was going to the condo he and Dali had in Manhattan. I had a lot of questions to ask, but I didn't want to push him any further over the edge than he already was.

It wasn't until a few days later that he told me the whole story. Told me of how Dali had come to him with the confession of cheating with another partner at her firm. He told me of how she felt she had to tell him the truth, especially since she was pregnant and didn't know if he was the father.

"Diego, you know me. And you know how much pride I took in my marriage. I took pride in my wife and the home we'd built. So for her to fuck another man hurt me like I ain't never been hurt before. And then to tell me she's pregnant and the kid could have been his took the cake."

"How did you find out it wasn't yours?" I'd asked him while we sat in the office after work.

"She took an early DNA test because there was no way I could wait nine months to know if the child she was carrying was mine or not."

"And I take it the test told you it wasn't yours."

He glanced out his office window, then thumbed his nose as he shook his head.

That had been a month ago. That was why Carl's actions, while questionable, didn't surprise me. Any other time his actions would have been odd to me, but because I knew he was having trouble at home, him paying attention to another woman just told me he was doing what he had to do to move on. Carl had never cheated on his wife. Hell, he didn't even flirt with other women because he took his vows seriously. He'd come from a single-mother home, and he vowed that he would never bring children into the world unless he was a husband first. I had a hell of a lot of respect for the man my best friend was.

I checked the time on my watch while Shell and Gabby whispered back and forth. I didn't know what they were talking about, but I could guess. I didn't need to talk to Carl to know what he was thinking. I'd initially only walked over to their table because Carl had wanted to talk to Shell. He'd been checking her out for quite some time, since she had walked in the door, actually.

Even still, I found myself more than thrilled to have to take one for the team. Taking one for the team between male friends usually meant while one friend tried his luck with the pretty girl, the other friend kept the less attractive friend occupied. Turned out that Shell's friend was just as beautiful as she was. I couldn't front like her backside in the dress she was wearing wasn't holding my attention. Baby may have been a little on the short side, but she had a body that could weaken any man.

She had just the right amount of everything, I surmised, as we walked back inside. I chuckled. I had to. Gabby had given her friend, Shell, a strong side eye when we walked back in to find she and Carl locked in a battle of the tongues again. Gabby sat down and looked at her glass of wine as if something was wrong with it before pushing it away. While I didn't know why she'd done that, it was safe to assume it was because she didn't want to end up like her friend, tonguing down a stranger.

"So are you going to give me that dance we talked about, or are you going to keep cock blocking Shell?" I asked Gabby in jest.

She turned to me, then blinked slowly. "I am *not* cock blocking," she said with a light laugh.

"Looks like it to me," I told her.

"Whatever," she quipped saucily. "Forgive me for making sure my friend doesn't lose herself in lust."

"But what if she wants to?"

Carl placed a kiss on Shell's neck. Shell really looked as if she was helpless to the seduction Carl was putting on her. No way should a married woman leave home unsatisfied in such a way that a married man, not her husband, should have that look of pure lust in her eyes.

Gabby shook her head and sighed. "She's grown."

"Yes, she is," I replied. "What goes on, on the island, stays on the island."

I took in Gabby's beauty under the soft glow of the lights. Her lips made me wonder what they would feel like on mine. I stood and held my hand out for her to take. She smiled, left my jacket in the booth and her clutch in Shell's possession. To be honest, Shell hadn't been paying much attention to us since she and Carl were glued into whatever conversation they were having.

I took Gabby's hand and led her onto the dance floor. The band was playing something with a catchy beat. It wasn't fast enough for us to throw our hands in the air and get down, but it wasn't slow enough to make the lovers in the room swoon to either. We moved through the throng of dancers and found a spot to settle in to.

I placed my hands on her waist while she placed hers on my chest.

"This is pretty awkward for me," she said.

"What is?"

"Dancing."

"You don't dance?"

"Oh, I dance. I just don't dance with men so much taller than I am."

I gave a grin and nodded. Even in the heels she had on, I was still towering over her.

"That's too bad. I like my women short so this feels just fine to me."

She giggled lightly. "You have an answer for everything, don't you?"

"I do like to be prepared for anything."

"How does that work out for you?"

"I've never been caught unprepared."

"I see."

"See what?"

"You think you're smooth. Think you can get me with your play on words."

I chuckled while gazing down at her. "Play on words? What do you mean?"

"You know exactly what I mean."

I held eye contact with her. Couldn't get the way her brown eyes held that hint of a challenge. She was feisty.

"Can't stand the heat?"

"What heat?" she asked coolly, but the smirk on her face told me she could give as good as she got.

"Oh, I see. You're trying to say my game is weak?"

"Nope. Just wanted to hear you admit you were gaming."

"And I always play to win."

She shook her head, then closed the gap a little more between us as we moved to the beat. My hands slipped down to the small of her back. The temptation to run my hand over the swell of her ass was so strong I had to talk myself out of it. I wasn't a man who couldn't control his urges, but there was just something about her that pulled at everything that made me male. I moved her closer still. I was surprised at how easily she lay her head against my chest.

We stayed that way until one song gave way to another. The smooth jazz sounds of Eugene Wilde betrayed what I was thinking. *If I could get her home with me tonight* . . . I chuckled to myself. It had been a minute since I'd had a one-night stand. The satisfying thrill of the rush intrigued me. She was a stranger, one who I wouldn't mind slipping into just to see if she moved underneath me the way she easily glided against me.

And she could Step. The heels she had on didn't slow her down. She kept in time with my stylish moves. We would have made Chicago Steppers a little jealous with the way we were grooving. I could tell she was all in. She stepped back, threw her hands up, did a spin, then slid back in to me with a hip roll. She was being playful, teasing me with her eyes and the pucker of her lips.

I couldn't help it; my eyes followed her ass like I was the negative to her positive. She knew it. That was why she turned around and looked back at me as she moved seductively. Her seductive play made me wonder if she had only been trying to keep Shell on the straight and narrow so she wouldn't be tempted to be led astray as well.

Looked like Shell had already been led somewhere, though. I glanced over to see that she and Carl were nowhere to be found. I stepped in the name of seduction. Pulled Gabby against me, her backside pushing against me. I knew she could feel what her presence was doing to me. I didn't try to hide it either. I showed her why the Cuban, African, and Puerto Rican in me blended so well. I worked my hips in time with hers. Felt when her breathing changed, deepened. She did a swift turn in my arms, and before she could say anything, my lips found hers. I nibbled on the corners of her mouth, urging her to let me in. I had the urge to pick her up since dipping my head to her level wasn't giving me what I wanted. She stiffened at first, then relaxed once my tongue flicked against her lips. She stood on her toes to help me out. I kept my hands on her hips as I kissed her. Kept rocking to the tune while we kissed like lovers and not strangers.

She kissed me like she was famished for that kind of affection. She wasn't a novice to the art of kissing. I knew by the way her hands curved around my neck and by the way she tilted her head to take the kiss deeper. She sucked my tongue like she had forgotten we were in a room full of people. I returned the kiss like I didn't give a damn one way or the other.

Chapter 8

Carl

It's been said that black men can't be faithful, that we're all cheaters, liars, and flat-out dogs. Well, in my case, that couldn't have been further from the truth. For seventeen years, I was the exception to the alleged rule. Not once did I even look at another woman, let alone sleep with one. I doted over my wife . . . gave her any and everything she ever wanted.

She wanted to move to Long Island, I moved, even though it lengthened my commute to the office considerably. She wanted a half million-dollar house built from the ground up, she got it. She wanted to lease a new car every single year, it was hers. Trips to Paris, Milan, Monaco, I made them happen. Whatever Dalisay desired, Dalisay got. Why? Simply because I loved my wife, and her happiness meant everything to me. Dammit, I knew I was a good black man, and no one could tell me different.

But I realized my love wasn't enough when I discovered that my wife was fucking her coworker, and now she was having his baby. The only reason she ended up confessing that scandalous shit in the first place was because she planned on keeping the child; otherwise, she could have simply gotten rid of it, and I would have been none the wiser. Dali was about eight weeks into the pregnancy when she came clean. I couldn't even tell that she was pregnant. She gave me some bullshit excuse about her and John working long hours together, and things just *happened*. Hell, many times I worked long hours too, but you didn't see me fucking my secretary! Unlike my lying, cheating, whore of a wife, I actually believed in, and honored, my marriage vows.

I wanted to choke the life out of her ass right then and there, but realized I couldn't. At least, not until I found out whether the baby she was carrying was mine. Thank God for a DNA blood test. Not only was it almost 100 percent accurate, it could be done as early as eight weeks, which meant hers was done right away. I admit, I did want the baby to be mine. I had always wanted children, and, at first, so did Dali, but as time passed, and she advanced further in her career, she came up with more and more excuses as to why the timing wasn't right. Back then, I had let it go. I didn't want her to think her career wasn't important, because it was. In fact, I was extremely proud of my wife; was her biggest supporter. She had made partner at her law firm and had legitimately worked her way up to being a successful attorney in her own right.

From the time we first met in college, I just knew there was something about her. Yes, her beauty was striking. Her skin held just the hint of a natural tan. She was taller than most Filipino woman, standing at five feet seven, and had the body of a Victoria's Secret model. But it was more than that; she had a brain in her head and the confidence to match her looks. That was a turn-on for me.

From the jump, Diego wasn't too fond of her, saying she was just looking for her next meal ticket, but he tolerated her for the sake of our friendship. Before we got together, Dali had dated a Heisman trophy candidate, a basketball player slated to enter the NBA draft, the student body president, and a few others who appeared to be going places.

And then there was me, a guy, who, along with Diego, had not only earned coveted internships with Apple, but also jobs with the company once we graduated. Diego and I had worked on some new technology during our internship that actually earned several patents, as well as millions of dollars, for the company. This paved the way for us to write our own tickets into Apple. Dali knew I was headed for big things, and she wanted to be right there with me. I was all for it, because I knew she had big plans of her own. She was an honor student who worked hard, so I knew she wasn't just riding on my coattails. I felt that she was an ambitious woman who wanted a man just as ambitious, and I respected that.

But every ounce of respect I once had for her died when I found out about her betrayal. I couldn't understand how someone who had everything could just throw it all away. She had a good man, a good life, and she discarded it like yesterday's garbage. She tried to tell me it was all a huge mistake and she still loved me. How could she let another man not only fuck her, but fuck her raw and in *my* bed, and say she still loves me? How could she carry that son-of-a-bitch's child, and still love me? Love, my black ass!

I was willing to forgive her, give her another chance if the baby had been mine. Hell, I had even considered doing the same if the baby wasn't mine and she got rid of it. But when we found out it wasn't mine, and she adamantly refused to terminate the pregnancy, I lost it. I'd be damned if I was going to stay with a cheating slut pregnant by the next man. If it hadn't been for Diego coming to the house to stop me, that tramp might not be alive today.

As it stood, I couldn't stay in the same house with her. I couldn't stand the sight of Dali. I was that disgusted with her. Couldn't stand to watch her belly growing as she was carrying another man's seed. I moved permanently to the condo I owned in Manhattan and filed for a divorce with a quickness. I even went so far as to have her served at work for all her coworkers to see, and even though I wasn't there to observe the deed myself, the scathing call I received from her let me know I got my point across. Her voice was laced with venom as she relayed how embarrassed she was when the messenger delivered the divorce papers and said, "You've been served," just as she was finishing up a presentation with the entire firm in attendance. Welcome to my world, bitch!

The acid in her tone intensified when she read the part of the papers stating that either she had to buy me out of the house we once shared, or it had to be sold, with the proceeds split accordingly. While Dali made a nice salary, I knew she in no way had the funds to buy me out, which meant as soon as the house was sold, she needed to find another place for her and her unborn bastard child to live. Let her go live with her baby daddy. I didn't care. Either way, I was done with her. Seventeen fucking years of my life wasted!

So here I was, still dealing with the bitterness, the anger, and the resentment I'd harbored since the day that trifling bitch dropped an atomic bomb on me. If it wasn't for Diego reining me in and constantly reminding me that jail wasn't a good look, I would have gone off the deep end weeks ago. Instead, right now, I was silently drowning my sorrows with a voluptuous, dark skinned beauty, a woman the complete opposite of Dali. Someone who appeared to be just as troubled as I was.

Shell and I exited the club and walked a short distance to the rear parking lot where the ladies' rented Dodge Journey sat. Shell had the keys. She pressed a button, deactivating the alarm, then maneuvered herself to sit on the hood of the car. I stood in front of her, planting myself between her legs, which seemed to open reflexively, my hands resting on the hood. Looking into her eyes, I saw a sadness that most certainly resembled my own. I didn't think she'd mind if I asked why.

"Why are you so unhappy?"

She gazed at me for a long moment, as if contemplating whether she should answer me. Finally, she replied, "It's not that I'm unhappy, I'm just not as happy as I could be."

"Bullshit," I countered.

"What?" Her eyes locked with mine, seeking clarification of my comment.

"I said bullshit. If you were even the slightest bit happy, you wouldn't be locking lips with me. Which tells me that your life back home is no fairy tale."

Shell broke her gaze with me, staying quiet for a few minutes. I had hit a nerve for sure. When she did answer, she tried to deflect what I said back on to me. "Well, from where I'm sitting, your life must not be a fairy tale either since you're here sucking face with me."

Ouch! She was right. My life used to be like a fairy tale, the stuff legends were made of. Now, it was just a fractured one, and, like Humpty Dumpty, that shit couldn't be put back together again.

Shell didn't stop there. "Why did you take your ring off?"

I chortled sarcastically. "As far as I'm concerned, I'm not married anymore."

"Why? What did she do?"

"What did your husband do to make you so unhappy?"

"Can you just answer the question, Carl?"

"You first."

She sighed, undoubtedly exasperated with me. "Long story short, I caught him cheating on me in our home, with my kids within earshot. Then he left us and moved in with the cunt-bag whore. And you want to know the worst part?" She didn't wait for me to respond. "I'm the damn fool wondering if I did anything to cause him to cheat. Stupid, right?"

I raised an eyebrow. Like so many women who discovered their partner was cheating, Shell was blaming herself for the fuckups made by the asshole she was married to. While we appeared to be kindred spirits dealing with the same type of pain, I'd be damned if I even remotely entertained the thought that Dalisay's cheating was in any way my fault.

"I wouldn't say stupid so much as . . . *misguided*. You can't blame yourself for what your husband did. Besides, what makes you think any of it was your fault?"

"I don't know," she started, staring off in the distance. "It's . . . he . . . I just can't do anything right by him. Nothing. And I feel trapped. Can't do anything; can't go anywhere without it leading to an argument. I can't even go to school without him trying to make me feel guilty. He makes me feel like a failure as a wife and a mother. I can't help but think I'm partially responsible in some way."

I couldn't believe the load of crap I was hearing. Shell married a real winner. It sounded to me like he ran some psychological bullshit on her and had her completely brainwashed. She almost sounded like someone who was held captive by a kidnapper, and later sympathized with him or her. What was it called? Oh yes, *Stockholm syndrome*. He truly did a number on her.

"Let me get this straight; you're married to a complete and total jackass who's not supportive, who's holding you back, and let's not forget he cheated on you, so why not leave?" I asked, needing to know her motivation for staying in such a fucked relationship.

"I can't. We have two children together, and I can't afford to leave. Besides, despite it all, I still love my husband. Yes, we have major problems, but at the end of the day, it's for better or worse, right?" The weak smile on her face belied how she really felt.

Ours was definitely a case of misery loving company—with some stark differences. For one, I no longer loved nor cared about the woman who still bore my last name. And unlike Shell, I had both the ability and the resources to leave without so much as a thought. Lastly, I didn't have the encumbrance of children, something I once desperately wanted with Dalisay, but now was grateful never happened.

"I can understand you wanting to keep your family together, but staying because you have children doesn't always work."

"I know, but I don't want my kids growing up without their father. Despite everything, he is still a good dad."

I felt where she was coming from. I grew up without a father. I was the oldest child; had a mother who had six children by five different men. She was only fifteen when she had me. By the time she had my youngest brother at the age of forty, I was so fed up with her that I made her get her tubes tied. One would think that an overgrown woman her age would have known how to fucking use protection. I had to end up being responsible for everyone, *including* my mother; still am to this day. But even though I didn't have a father, in my opinion, I think I turned out pretty well.

"I get it, believe me I do, but just because both parents are in the home doesn't mean things will get any better, especially if one of the parents is the cause of the problems in the first place. And sorry to say this, but a good father doesn't screw his side pussy while his kids are in earshot, nor does he leave his kids for her."

"Carl, what happened between you and your wife?"

Obviously, she was tired of discussing her marriage, and it was apparent that she wasn't going to stop until she found out what caused the demise of mine.

"Do you really want to know?"

"Can you fucking stop answering my questions with more questions? Please?"

I hated rehashing this shit, but it was the least I could do considering she told me about her jacked-up marriage.

"Bottom line, my cheating whore of-a-wife was fucking her coworker, and now she's having his baby."

She covered her mouth, as in disbelief. "Oh my gosh, Carl, I am *so* sorry."

"Why? You didn't do it. That soon-to-be ex-slut I have the displeasure of being married to did."

I felt the bile rising in my throat at the thought of Dalisay.

"Well, I still feel bad. You're divorcing her?"

"Yes, and the sooner the better."

"How could she do that to you? How could she get pregnant with another man's child?" Shell asked, like I had the answer to that question.

"I don't know. You'd have to ask her," I replied, more sarcastically than I should have.

"Can I ask you one more question?" she asked cautiously. I was guessing it was because she picked up on my snarky behavior.

"Yes, but only one more, and that's it."

"Have you ever cheated on your wife?"

"Never. Have you ever cheated on your husband?"

"No," she replied, lowering her eyes as if in shame.

I wasn't trying to make her feel bad, but the same way she wanted to know, I wanted to know too.

"So why do you want to now?" I stood there patiently waiting for an answer that wouldn't come. "Look, as far as I'm concerned, I'm not married anymore. Like I told you before, she doesn't matter to me. Does your husband matter to you?"

In a whisper, she said, "Yes."

I lifted her chin with my finger, forcing her to look at me. My lips took hers, hands wandering to her ample hips, then to her full breasts. I parted her lips with my tongue, inviting myself into her mouth. A moan escaped from her throat. I pulled her closer to me, heat emanating from between her thighs. Pressing myself into her, I allowed her to feel what I was working with; that part of me that wished we weren't separated by something as trivial as clothing. Yeah, her mouth said her husband mattered, but her body was saying something entirely different.

Shell pulled back, her breathing hitched. "Carl, why? Why me?" Her self-esteem issues clearly evident.

I had been completely honest with her, and I wasn't about to start lying now.

I looked her in the eyes and said, "Because I want you."

Chapter 9

Mischelle

I stood there looking at the man in front of me. We had come to a standstill. I'd invited him back to the house, inside of my personal space. Yet, I didn't think I could go through with the actual act of having sex with him. The room was dark, the only light was by the moon. The large bay windows were open and the nightlife of Tybee Island serenaded us. Storm clouds were rolling in as light rain started to fall. Downstairs, we'd left Gabby and Diego to their own devices.

Nervousness settled into my spine as I stood between Carl's legs while he sat on the edge of the bed. Gone were his shirt, slacks, socks, and shoes. All he had on were on his black boxer briefs that did little to hide his arousal. He mindlessly rubbed my thighs while he placed kisses against my stomach. I didn't have abs. Years of bad eating and minimal exercising had added fluffiness where flat planes should have been. Carl didn't seem to care though. All he'd wanted me to do was say yes . . . .

"Because I want you."

Those had been the words that started it all. His words echoed loudly in my mind as he went back in for another kiss. He and I were outside. I was sitting on the hood of the rented truck. I had to admit, I was lost in the moment. I didn't know why, out of all the women in the small jazz club, he chose me. I wasn't going to act like I wasn't thrilled at the notion he had chosen me. I mean, they didn't grow men like Carl in Atlanta. Well, that was a lie. They grew them like Carl in Atlanta. It was just that those like Carl were attracted to the other men who looked like Carl.

Then, there was my husband. I sighed inwardly while Carl's hands explored my thighs and ass. Malik had basically forgotten what it was to romance me. Not that he'd been a big romancer to begin with, but at least he used to tell me how proud he was that I was his wife. Now, I got nothing. But, to be honest, I was tired of Malik taking over my weekend. Even though he was nowhere to be found physically, mentally, he'd been occupying my mind the whole trip thus far.

I let all thoughts of him go when Carl started to undo the buttons on my blouse. My breasts had already been put on display because of the sheer fabric, but that didn't seem to be enough for Carl. His big hands roamed over the swell of my breasts before he released them from their laced barriers. I was nervous. I couldn't lie. Was holding my breath until I felt his lips wrap around my nipples. I glanced around quickly before my eyes rolled into the back of my head. I wanted to make sure no one would catch us in the hedonistic act.

The back parking lot wasn't as crowded as the one nearest the club. Gravel crunched under Carl's shoes anytime he moved. Gabby had parked near the rear in a spot that wouldn't get us blocked in when it was time to leave. Low-hanging trees above hid us partially while the faint sounds of the ocean blended in with my heated moans and bated breaths.

I could feel his manhood trying to free itself from his imprisoned zipper. Found my hips rolling on their own while my back arched to give him easier access. I couldn't remember the last time a man had paid equal attention to both my breasts. Carl went from one to the other, licking, sucking, and tugging my nipples with teeth while he massaged my breasts . . . used the flat of his tongue in lapping motions all around the softest areas of them.

I reached for him, popped the buttons open on his shirt, then let my hands explore every part of his chiseled chest and abs. I could tell by looking at the way his shirt fit him that he spent a great deal of time in the gym, but actually being able to see them was a different thing altogether.

What in hell was I doing? I thought while I tugged the ends of his shirt free from his slacks. He stopped the nipple play, then admired his work just as I admired the firmness of his abs. They clenched under my intense gaze. The perfectly symmetrical V shape made me want to see how many licks it would take to get him to come.

I was way out of my element, but I didn't want to be reeled back in. I wanted to unbuckle his belt, slip my hands into his pants, and see if what was there looked as good as it felt pressed against my heat.

His tongue ran over his lips before he said to me, "What will it take to get you and me in the same room tonight?"

I knew what he was asking, but I was too embarrassed to come right out and tell him he could follow me back to my rented house on the beach so we could finish what we started.

"We can go back in the club," I told him, jokingly. "We'd be in the same room together again."

I smiled. He chuckled . . . gave my breasts a little more attention before approaching female giggles and male laughter forced him to stop. While he made sure my breasts had been hidden and blouse was buttoned, he *didn't try to adjust his opened shirt. He took my hand and helped me from the hood of the truck. My legs were a bit weak from the tension of the moment. My lace boyshorts moved around a bit uncomfortably because of the wetness soaking them.*

"What would you think of me if I had sex with you hours after meeting you?" I asked him.

I was a bit self-conscious about acting like a full-blown wanton brazen whore.

"I would think you were a woman in control of her sexual desires."

"You wouldn't think I was tramp like your wife?" I asked. He grunted, then looked out over the area as if he was in thought. I continued, "I mean, after all, I'm a married woman too."

Carl turned his attention back to me, pushed the ends of his shirt back, then slid his hands into his pockets. To be honest, after that small gesture, I didn't even remember what I had been asking him. The way his chest and abs sat chiseled like they had been carved out of stone had stolen my ability to form a complete thought. For a minute, under his intense gaze, my throat went dry. Hands started to sweat. All the moisture I had inside of me pooled to the seat of my panties.

Behind those thin, black-framed glasses was a look so primal and penetrating, it was almost animalistic. I bit down on my bottom lip as butterflies settled into the pit of my stomach. The wind started to make the leaves on the trees rock in a lazy, spellbinding dance.

"First of all, I don't know you well enough to call you a whore for your actions. And if you didn't have some apprehension that would bother me. Your reluctance to continue tells me you're not a woman who goes around slanging pussy to all suitors. All I see is a beautiful woman having the time of her life, and I'm offering her another

way to live out a fantasy. For tonight, we can pretend I'm your husband and you're my wife. You've never cheated on me. I've never cheated on you, and I'm aiming to do whatever it takes to make you happy again," he said, as he closed the gap between us again. His arms snaked around my waist; then his hands so elegantly palmed my ass. "All you have to do is say yes . . ."

And I did. I said yes. We headed back the club to search for Gabby who was already on her way out searching for me. Once she got done reading me my rights about running off without saying a word with a stranger I'd just met, I told her I wanted Carl.

"People want a lot of things—that doesn't mean they have to have them," she quipped.

"Well, for once, I'm going to go for what I want, and I want him."

She cast a glance behind me at Diego and Carl.

"You sure you want to do this?" she asked me.

I nodded. "I'm sure."

"And I guess I'm supposed to entertain his friend while you and he play hide-and-go-get."

I smiled, then gave Diego an up-and-down appreciative look. "You should be trying to climb that mighty sequoia."

She couldn't hold her laughter. "What?" she blurted out.

I laughed with her. "You heard me. Climb, Gabby, climb."

We both had a good laugh. Diego was a tall, strapping brother. His mixed heritage had brought out the best of both cultures in him. He was no slouch, and Gabby would be crazy to let all that slip away without at least a sample. Honey-golden eyes, strong chin with that perfect Werther's Original complexion, and a gait that made even me swoon. Normally, men

his height had a kind of goofy disposition in the way
they carried themselves, but not Diego. He stood like
he'd invented GQ, same as Carl.

"I don't normally do this kind of crap, and you know
this, but for you, I'll look the other way," she said, finally
agreeing to my terms.

I stood quiet for a minute. Couldn't believe I was
about to partake in a one-night stand. The thought
of what would happen if my husband ever found out
almost made me change my mind. However, another
look over at Carl made me throw caution to the wind.

Now my nervousness had gotten the better of me. I
wanted to back off. Felt the urge to go back on that yes
and tell him no. But he was sitting in front of me damn
near naked. Underneath that expensive suit he wore
showed there was more to Carl than met the eye. His suit
had hidden the Kemetian tribal tattoo that covered his
upper back. On his neck was an ankh tattoo while his arm
boasted of the brand that told he'd pledged purple and
gold. This man was a walking African god if I ever saw
one, thick and sinewy with muscle.

He stood, and I found myself trying hard to breathe.
I inhaled so hard my chest started to hurt. Was I really
about to cheat on my husband? Should I even care at
this point? There was a lump in my throat as I absent-
mindedly ran a hand through my braids. No, two wrongs
didn't make a right, but, for once, I was thinking about
doing something that would make *me* happy.

"Carl?" I called out to him just to slow down the moment.

"Shell."

"What if we—what if we do this and neither one of us
likes it?"

"There is always that possibility, but I'm guessing that
you already know that won't be the case."

Thunder boomed through the heavens right as lightning ripped across the sky. I jumped. Carl chuckled.

"You're nervous, and that's fine. If you don't want to do anything, just say so."

Easier said than done, I thought. My body was craving something that I hadn't had in over a year. My husband used to make me come, and he used to be very skilled in the oral sex department, but something had been missing as of late. I was always left needing more.

That didn't matter, though. Carl lifted me from the floor just as a strong wind blew into the room carrying a mist of rain behind it. He gently eased me onto the middle of the bed. I arched and moaned when he eased my underwear to the side, then let two of his long, thick fingers slip inside of me. My vaginal walls enclosed around his fingers. Eyelids fluttered when he expertly started to move them in and out of me.

"*Hmmmm,*" I gasped.

"Damn," he murmured. "So wet and tight."

He removed his fingers, urged me to lift my hips so he could drag my boyshorts down until he tossed them behind him. Kneeling down at the foot of the bed, he pulled me to him. Before I could brace myself for what was to come, he placed gentle kisses against my lips and pearl. Did that like he knew the ins and outs of my desires. He took his time while letting his tongue slip between my folds. There was nothing like a man who knew how to practice the art of oral sex.

My hands gripped the green comforter on the bed, then found his braided locs to hold him in place against my clitoris. My hips lifted from the bed to keep up with the intense pleasure he was giving me. I could only hope the roar of the storm could hide the cries of pleasure erupting from me. I rolled my hips in sync with the movements of his head. Felt myself about to release like never before. It had been so long since I'd had an orgasm that I was sure I was about to explode.

Just before I did, though, Carl pulled back. He stepped out of his boxer briefs and blessed me with the gift of sight. My eyes widened at the sight of his manhood. The long, thick, two-toned work of art was riddled with veins. I had a thing for dicks with visible veins. Meant the blood flow there was without obstruction. And it was clear where all the blood had rushed in Carl's body. When his dick bobbed up and down, I blew out air.

I watched as he grabbed the golden-wrapped condom, ripped it open, then slid it on. There was something sexy about a man putting on a condom. I couldn't explain it, but seeing a man take his safety just as seriously as I took mine turned me on. My eyes watched him as he crawled onto the bed, caged me between his arms, and then brought his lips back down to mine. His kiss had been a distraction. He kissed me so the surprise of his head breaking skin wouldn't cause me to lose my mind. God, he felt so damn good. I broke the kiss when I gasped out for air. Tiny whimpers of pain and pleasure told of my satisfaction.

"Oh shit," I breathed out.

As he slinked deeper into me, he held eye contact. It was the most intense thing I'd ever experienced. I didn't know if he was really pretending I was his wife, and at that point, I didn't care. All I knew was when his hips started to rock against mine, everything seemed right in my world. It wasn't a slow groove, but it wasn't a fast one. It was one that told me he was looking for pleasure and aching to give it in return.

His breathing intensified with each stroke. I made sure to fight through my walls stretching to accommodate him. I forgot about the slight pain and focused on the deep pleasure. Carl was so deep, I couldn't tell where he ended and I began. His hands gripped mine and held them over my head before he moved his hands back down to hold my thighs. From my eyes, to my ears, to my lips, Carl kissed me. He didn't forget about my nipples either.

He watched me as he long stroked me. Like a predator stalking its prey, one toying with his dinner before he ate it, Carl used his short strokes to keep me dangling over the edge. One would have thought it was my first time having sex in a while. That wasn't the case. This was what I had been missing, and it was what I needed. Carl was giving me what I wanted. Thickness. Length. He was hitting those spots that had never been touched, ones that I'd craved. Ones my husband hadn't cared to explore.

He pushed deeper, harder.

"Shit, Carl . . ."

He grunted low. Gave a guttural groan of his own.

"Your fault, Shell. Shouldn't be so damn good."

I crooned out for him, sang a song of satisfaction with a melody of moans. He kneeled back on his haunches, hooked the back of my knees into the creases of his elbows, and lifted my ass from the bed. Blinding lights crashed against my eyes. Muscles clenched so hard in my abdomen that it almost hurt. I bit down on my bottom lip while my feet arched and flexed in response to the oncoming orgasm. I could hear the sea rocking outside my windows just as waves of my satisfaction made me hyperventilate.

Carl's upper lip twitched. Creases in his head foreshadowed his tide coming in.

"Come for me," he demanded.

My head fell back when his hips beat against mine reminding me of wild African drums. I came for him. I came so hard that when I felt him swell and get harder inside of me, I pumped my hips harder against his. I *needed* this. I needed *la petite mort*. Chased that little fucker until he took us both down for the count.

Chapter 10

Gabrielle

I couldn't believe Shell talked me into bringing these men back to the beach house. They were two complete strangers, and even though we had checked them out, anything could still happen. But I had to face facts; she was a grown woman and was going to do whatever she wanted regardless of what I said. She knew what she wanted, as well as the consequences of her actions, and I couldn't have stopped her. And Lord knows I tried! As it stood, as soon as we walked through the door, Shell and Carl headed straight for her bedroom. They couldn't get there fast enough. What they were doing was anybody's guess, while I was left alone to entertain Diego.

Sure, he seemed really nice; he was funny, handsome, smart, educated, charming, light on his feet, and was a really good kisser, but I still felt a bit uncomfortable being alone with a man I had just met hours before. My mind wandered back to the part about him being a good kisser. He caught me off guard when he kissed me on the dance floor at the club. But then again, I couldn't remember the last time I had been kissed. Daniel and I had broken up six months ago, but if I really think about the last time I had been kissed, I mean kissed with any real passion, it had to be about a year ago, when I had last slept with him. Maybe longer if I really thought about it.

For me, kissing and sex were intertwined, and although I couldn't pinpoint exactly when, my needs became less and less important to Daniel. Eventually, it seemed like all he wanted to do was gets his rocks off, and once he did, he was done. And it wasn't just in the bedroom where he fell short; he completely dropped the ball in all areas of our relationship. I tolerated him and his antics for many years until I had had enough. I would have preferred to remain celibate than to settle for mediocre intimacy at the hands of someone who couldn't have cared less. And I did—for an entire year; a very *long* year.

I had been dealing with my celibacy well enough until Diego kissed me, until he opened up something within me that I had thought was dead and buried; that part of me that longed for some real romance. Unfortunately, I didn't see that happening; not tonight or any time in the near future. If anything, at most, I'd end up having a one-night stand, and that was something I didn't do . . . had never done, for that matter, let alone with someone I had just met. Besides, I didn't want Diego's first impression of me to be one of an easy female he met on his weekend at Tybee Island. With his good looks and charm, I was quite sure he had come across many, many women like that in his lifetime.

I sighed, trying to clear my head. It was close to two in the morning, but I was far from tired.

"Can I offer you something to drink?" I asked Diego as I walked into the kitchen.

"What do you have?"

Looking in the refrigerator and the cabinets, I replied, "Juice, water, wine."

When I turned back around to look at him, I could have sworn Diego was checking me out, but then again, it could have easily been my imagination.

"Wine will do."

I grabbed a bottle of Il Duca Imperiale 1917 Stella Rosa Rosso grape wine out of the cabinet and handed the bottle, along with the corkscrew I fished out of a drawer, to him. I took two wineglasses from the rack and motioned for Diego to follow me. The rain was coming down at a steady pace, making the already chilled night air even colder. Despite that, I led him to the screened-in porch, but not before grabbing an oversized, fluffy blanket from the linen closet near the bathroom. The heated hot tub provided some warmth and just enough light to see, but not enough to be distracting, while the large couch and loveseat made the atmosphere very inviting. I opted for the coziness of the loveseat.

Diego poured wine into the glasses that I had placed on the end table next to the love seat. Before I made myself comfortable, I took off his jacket and handed it back to him; then I sat on the loveseat, covering myself with the blanket. He put the jacket on, sat down, then picked up both glasses, handing one to me. I took a slow sip of the sweet liquid. It tasted good and made me feel a little bit warmer as it ran down my throat.

"Can I ask you question?" I inquired, taking another taste of liquid courage.

"Sure, feel free," he replied, savoring his glass.

"How come someone like you, a man who is smart, funny, very successful, and pretty easy on the eyes, isn't married yet? I'm sure there are plenty of women who'd give their right arm, and probably the left one as well, to be Mrs. Diego Lopez-Hernandez," I said, remembering his full name from his business card.

He laughed. "So you think I'm pretty easy on the eyes, huh?"

I shook my head, laughing with him. "Out of that entire question, that's *all* you heard? Yes, Diego, you are quite nice to look at. Now answer the question, please."

"To be honest with you, half the time, I don't know if a woman wants to be with me, or wants to be with me for my money. Frankly, I haven't met the woman I want to marry yet, and I possibly never will."

I appreciated where he was coming from. Someone like him definitely had to be on guard for the gold diggers of the world, and I'm sure he came across them frequently. "I understand, but never say never. I'm pretty sure one day you'll meet the woman who will make an honest man out of you," I teased.

"Maybe, but I doubt it. And for the record, I'm always honest; some people can't handle my brand of honesty," he quipped, as he refilled my empty wineglass. "On that same note, I could ask you the same question."

I gladly accepted a second helping of the sweet red liquid libation. "My ex and I weren't married, but it was like a marriage."

"Playing married and being married are two different things."

"This coming from a man who's never been married in the first place," I countered. "One thing is different, though. It's easier to walk away. No legalities once it's over, for the most part, unless you own property together or have kids."

"Point taken. If you don't mind me asking, how come you two never got married? Twelve years is a long time, after all."

It wasn't that I minded; I just got irritated with myself when I thought about the answer. "We got complacent, and I . . . settled. The years went by, and it was just easier to leave things the way they were. Plus, I guess that old phrase still applies; why buy the cow when you can get the milk for free? My fault for not pressing the issue as much as I should have. Anyway, it's over, so there's no use dwelling on it now. I can tell you this, though; there's no way I will ever wait again that long for someone to decide whether he wants to get married. That's assuming I ever let someone get that close to me again."

"Why did you two break up?" Diego queried, pouring himself another glass of wine.

"There were lots of reasons, main one being he took me for granted; thought he could treat me any kind of way, and I wouldn't go anywhere. Not that he was abusive or anything; he was just a jerk. For a long time I stuck around, until I finally wised up and realized I deserved much better." I shrugged.

From the look on his face, I could tell Diego knew he hit a sore spot with me. He quickly changed the subject. "Are you cold?"

"No," I replied. "Between the blanket, the steam from the hot tub, and the wine, I'm feeling pretty good. How about you?"

"I'm a bit chilly myself. Mind if we share your blanket? Don't be afraid. I don't bite . . . unless you want me too." A broad smile crossed his lips.

I didn't know why, but Diego amused me. Yes, I knew he was running game on me, but I didn't care. I was actually enjoying our little game of cat and mouse, with him being the very big cat on the prowl. I moved toward him, placing half of the blanket across his legs. I looked into his eyes, and before I knew it, Diego had once again stolen a kiss.

I should have seen that coming, but he caught me so off guard, I almost dropped my glass. He had already placed his on the end table. Still locked in kiss, he took mine, placing it there as well. He skillfully used his tongue, licking around my lips, parting them, his tongue finding mine. I had never been kissed like that before . . . felt such heat from something as simple as a kiss. I tasted the wine on his breath. I wanted more—*needed* more.

Before I knew it, Diego pulled me on top of him, straddling his legs. His hardness pressed against me, fueling a desire building within me. Grabbing a handful of my locs, his full, moist lips moved down my neck, stopping to suck on one spot. His big hands slowly moved up my legs, sending jolts of electricity through me. He lightly traced his fingers along my thighs until they reached my firm derrière. He slid his hands down the back of my lace cheeky panties, giving both of my round mounds a strong squeeze. I let out a soft moan.

My lips found his, our tongues dancing their own tango. As I moved against him, I felt a hardness; that part of him that contained a heartbeat all its own. It pulsated, emanating heat that I could feel through his pants. He groaned low in his throat. The wind shifted direction, with the rain now coming through the holes in the screen. Small drops of rain pelted us as we enjoyed the taste and feel of each other. It was only when I saw a flash of lightning and heard the boom of thunder seconds later that I knew it was time to take our private party elsewhere.

Without a word, I led Diego upstairs to my bedroom, stopping only long enough to grab a plastic bag I had left on the kitchen counter. The room was completely dark. Not wanting to turn on the lights and kill the mood, I, instead, turned on the television, searching for the smooth jazz channel. Once the music began to play, Diego resumed his seduction. He took off my heels and lifted me up onto the bed. I was now eye level with him. I stared for a long moment into those liquid honey eyes, wondering what this man would think of me once I gave myself to him. I could stop now before we took things too far. I could, but I wasn't sure I wanted to.

"I need to tell you something," I said, my heart beating fast.

His fingers were slowly working on the zipper on the back of my dress. "What is it?"

"I haven't been with anyone in a year."

"I thought you said you broke up with your boyfriend six months ago," he said matter-of-factly.

"I did, but I stopped sleeping with him long before we broke up. And just so you know, I've never, ever had a one-night stand."

He looked at me, as if seeking my eyes for the truth.

"In that case, thank you for letting me be your first. Don't worry, I won't judge you," he said with a grin.

Whatever reservations I had were gone, and I was his for the taking. Diego moved the spaghetti straps from my shoulders, allowing my dress to fall freely on the bed. He stepped back, surveying me. I felt as if I was on display.

"You are so beautiful," he said.

He moved in close again, scooping me up in his arms, giving me that thing that made my heart race . . . that kiss, that hot, sexy, passionate kiss. After he quickly took off his jacket and tossed it on a chair, I reached down to pull his Polo shirt from inside his pants, quickly pulling it up and over his head. Now it was my turn to ogle. From his broad, strong chest, down to his hard, washboard abs, the man standing in front of me was a sight to behold. I couldn't help but run my fingertips all the way from his chest down to his abs. When I lightly brushed my fingertips over his nipples, he let out a groan.

Picking me up as if I weighed nothing, he laid me down on the bed. I watched as he shed his pants, keeping on his black boxer briefs. The man had the faintest hint of body hair, which I found quite sexy. He gently covered me with his body. His hands reached underneath my back and adroitly unhooked my strapless black bra, tossing it to the side. He kissed from my lips down to my neck, then stopped to lick and suck on my erect nipples. His hands gently squeezed each of my perky breasts, his thumbs teasing my nipples.

He kissed lower, past my belly ring, until he reached my moist folds. He kissed and sucked in between my thighs, nibbled on my bud before removing my panties. His lips and tongue worked on my sensitive clit in tandem, sucking and licking, causing me to bite my lip for fear of moaning too loudly. I felt one finger enter me, moving in a *come hither* motion. My hands grabbed at the sheets as my legs wrapped around his neck. He removed his finger, licking my juices from it, replacing it with his long, thick tongue, French kissing my lips, making my walls shutter.

With his tongue still inside me and my legs around his neck, he reached his arms up underneath my back, lifting us both to a standing position. I held on for dear life as he backed me into a wall, his lips sucking on my lips and clit. I had never experienced anything like this before and probably never would again. But for the short time we were together, I was going to relish in each and every spine-tingling minute. With each thrust of his tongue I felt the tension building until, like the rain pouring outside in torrents, my flood gates opened, my juices freely flowing like Niagara Falls. He greedily sopped them up, like he had been in the desert and hadn't had water in days.

When he was done, he placed me back on the bed.

"That was sweet," he said, the sexiest smile on his face.

I couldn't help but giggle. Almost as if teasing me, he slowly removed his boxer briefs, and what I saw left me in amazement. He was *extremely* well endowed. Long, thick, wide. No one I had been with even came close to matching what Diego was packing. It was actually somewhat intimidating, but I had come too far to stop now.

He took out a condom and was about to open it when I noticed which brand it was. It was Trojans.

"Diego, wait," I said stopping him. "We can't use those."

"Why not?" he asked, pain in his expression.

"I'm allergic to them."

He looked defeated.

"But you can use these." I smiled, grabbing the bag I brought with me upstairs. I pulled out a box of Lifestyles Skyn Large condoms, opened it, and handed one to Diego. I was glad that Shell and I stopped at Kroger's on the way back to the house. A girl couldn't be too careful.

"A woman who's prepared. I like that," he said, ripping open the package, sheathing himself.

I lay back, anticipating what was to come. Once again, Diego covered me with his strong, hard body. I think he noticed the hesitation in my eyes, because he placed his lips close to my ear and whispered, "*Te prometo seré gentil*. I promise I'll be gentle."

He kissed me slowly, savoring the moment. Just as slowly, he began to enter me. Inch by excruciating inch, I felt him stretching my walls beyond capacity. A tear rolled from the corner of my eye. It hurt so much I wanted to cry out, but I bit on my bottom lip instead. I felt the pain all the way down my legs, up my back, and in my abdomen. I must have tensed up, because Diego stopped, wiping the tear from my eye.

"We can stop," he said.

"No, it's okay." I was lying through my teeth.

The pain was so intense I thought I'd need a coochie transplant by the time we were done. I expected it to be a bit painful, but I never expected anything like this.

"Are you sure?"

Instead of answering him, I kissed him hard, allowing him to continue his quest, until finally he filled me up. We stayed like that for a long moment, his member rhythmically pulsating inside of me. As promised, he was gentle, pulling almost all the way out of me, only to delve back in on a slow reentry. He sucked on my neck and my breasts, leaving passion marks along the way. Eventually, pain gave way to a mixture of pain and pleasure, but mostly pleasure. Diego started hitting spots within me that had my entire body shaking, had every single nerve ending on fire. I started moving with him, my fingertips digging into his back.

My moans egged him on as I began to match him, thrust for pleasure-driven thrust.

"*Sabía que podías tomar.* I knew you could take it," he said, the deep bass tone in his voice making me tingle all over.

I clenched my walls, making him close his eyes, a groan so deep coming from his throat it sounded like the distant rumble of thunder.

He found every spot that had me calling his name, and he would not stop. He was hurting me so good I didn't want him to stop.

"Right there?" he asked, paying attention to the way my body responded to each deep, hard, penetrating thrust.

"Yesssss," I replied on a whisper.

Diego should have been charged with assault with a deadly weapon for the things he was doing to me. The storm outside was nothing compared to the storm that was brewing within me.

As his thrusts became more rapid and more intense, his manhood grew in length and girth. I knew he was on the verge of coming, and he wasn't the only one. With pinpoint laser sharp accuracy, he ravished me over and over again until at just the right moment, we both exploded in carnal bliss.

Chapter 11

Diego

For some reason, as of late, it never failed that my phone would wake me up from my sleep. I could hear it vibrating on the nightstand beside the bed I was sharing with Gabby. I looked at the clock to see red block numbers glaring at me. Four thirty in the morning. I'd gotten in about an hour of sleep. I shook my head, then snatched my phone up to see Ricki had texted me.

You told me to text you to make sure you were awake, her text read.

That had been at four when the first text came through. I'd still been sleeping.

Diego, I'm going to call if you don't respond to this message just to make sure you're okay.

She was only doing what I'd asked her to do. Before plans had changed, I had every intention of being back at Hilton Head in the king-size bed afforded to me in the suite I had booked for the weekend. Between business meetings and sponsoring events for the Black Heritage Festival this weekend, I hadn't really had time to talk to her. Not that we talked on the phone a lot anyway. To be honest, I wasn't a phone person. I'd text more than talk. Would rather have a face-to-face conversation more so than bump my gums over the phone, unless business was involved, of course.

I knew Ricki had to be at work by five, so I told her to text to see if I was awake before she called me. She'd been at Duane Reade in Times Square for about two years.

I glanced over at Gabby resting peacefully beside me. Her locs fell down to cover her perky breasts while the white sheet covered the lower half of her body. Sex with her had been worth it, but as always, it took more than a nice body and good sex to keep my interest. Even though I've had my share of one-night stands, if a woman couldn't reel me in with her conversation within those first few minutes, then I would lose interest pretty quickly.

Gabby had kept my attention.

As I got up and headed to the bathroom, I thought about how many of my female friends complained that they didn't know me. They told me I only gave enough of myself to keep them hanging on, only enough to keep them hungry for more. They were right in some aspect. Anytime a woman got too close to me, I'd usually let her know it through actions. I'd ask her to stop calling so much and to not tell me her feelings because they wouldn't be reciprocated. Didn't need a woman in my personal space for more time than I wanted her to be.

Don't get me wrong, I'd tried the whole relationship shit, but it just wasn't for me. I wasn't in a hurry to get married either. I didn't have an aversion to marriage. Just wasn't in a rush to get down the aisle.

My father didn't understand why that was. He always teased me about the fact that Carl came from a broken home, no father, and no mother really, and yet, he had gotten married. I came from a home with loving parents. My father had always been a good husband to my mother. So they didn't get why I avoided relationships like the plague. People always thought there was some deep reason for it. To be honest, there wasn't. I didn't want to be tied down, plain and simple.

I finished paying the waterman, washed my hands, and then called Ricki.

"Hey, Swiper," she greeted, way too cheery for it to be four thirty in the morning.

Ricki's voice had always been calming. She had the kind of voice that could put a man's mind at ease after a long, hard day's work. Calling me Swiper was her play on the fact that Dora, the kiddy cartoon character on Nickelodeon, had a cousin named Diego. Now, I didn't know what Swiper the Fox had to do with Dora's cousin Diego, but I let Ricki get away with it. Simple things made her happy.

"Ricki, it's almost five in the morning. Why so damn lively?" I asked, my New York accent lagging with a bit of a drawl because I was still sleepy.

I grabbed the travel toothbrush Gabby had given me between the two rounds of sex we'd had. I found it comical that she knew I would be there long enough to have to use it. Regardless of all the talk she had done about not being a fan of one-night stands, she'd stopped at a store, purchased condoms, and a toothbrush. Women were funny like that. You didn't choose them; they chose you. I had yet to meet a woman who claimed to not do one-night stands and actually not participate in one. I didn't normally have to do or say too much. And not that I was bragging, but no woman I'd ever set my sights on had turned me down.

"Because I get my promotion today," she quipped.

I nodded as I remembered. "Ah, that's right. Lead pharmacy tech."

"That's right," she squealed with excitement. "You remembered! I worked so hard for this. I can help Mama with her bills more now."

"I put money in your account for that."

"I know, but I don't want to depend on you for my issues. I got it."

"Ricki," I said to her after I spit toothpaste in the sink, "I give you more than enough to handle her bills each month."

"So, it ain't your responsibility—"

"It's not yours either."

"She's my mother."

"And that means what—"

"So, how's your trip going, Swiper?"

She cut me off. It was her way of telling me she didn't want to talk about her mother's issues. Ricki had always taken care of her. While I didn't think she owed her mother anything, the woman had used guilt to get Ricki to do what she wanted. Telling your child she's the reason you had to drop out of high school to work in a shipyard so she could eat was a low blow. Ricki's mom had gotten sick while working there, and she loved to remind Ricki of it. On a few of the occasions that I'd taken her out, she had told me about it. Had even shed a few tears because of it.

"Going well."

"You did your booth thingy yet?"

"Booth thingy?"

She giggled. "Yeah, you know, the thing you're sponsoring."

"In a few hours."

"I miss you."

I looked into the mirror, then grabbed a clean towel to wipe my face. "Ricki."

She knew why I was calling her name. I didn't have to tell her to cut all that sappy, *I miss you shit,* at the pass. I examined my shoulders and saw the scratches where Gabby had dipped her nails into my skin.

Ricki backtracked. "I'm sorry."

It wasn't that I didn't appreciate the sentiment, but the last thing I wanted to do was have her expecting the same in return. No expressions of affection and she wouldn't have to worry about getting her feelings hurt when I didn't express the same feelings back to her. She knew the rules. I could tell by how quiet she'd gotten that I'd hurt her feelings. I could hear her Jillian Michaels DVD playing in the background. Ricki wasn't a fitness nut, but she did enough cardio and core training to keep her body in shape.

"So how's your trip going? You on your way out?" she asked before I could change the subject.

I grabbed a white towel and wet it with hot water. Washed my face. "Not right now. Chilling with a friend."

"Who, Carl?"

"No."

Just as I answered Ricki, a knock came on the bathroom door. I cracked it open to see Gabby standing there. Although she looked tired, she was still beautiful. She looked like a walking piece of art. Long locs cascaded down her back. Brown skin glowing. Thick, plush lips begging to be kissed again.

"Are you almost done?" Gabby asked me. "I need to use the bathroom."

I nodded and moved out of her way. I couldn't help but watch her ass jiggle in the little thin thigh-high gown she'd put on. I imagined what it would be like to slip back between those petite thighs. I grunted low in my throat when I remembered the pain she'd experienced upon first entrance. Couldn't believe she actually hadn't had sex in over a year. Pussy was tight and gushy. Warm and inviting.

"So is this a friend you just met or one you took with you?" Ricki asked out of the blue, throwing my thought process off.

I didn't doubt that she'd heard Gabby's voice, and her question was a way of trying to figure out who I was with and how much she meant to me.

I sighed, walked out of the bathroom, then closed the door behind me. "What the hell, Ricki?" I asked in a deep voice. "What're you playing at right now?"

"Sorry. Just making conversation."

"No, you're not."

"Yes, I am. Just asking stuff is all."

I grabbed my boxer briefs and pulled them on. Then I snatched my pants from the ottoman and made sure my wallet and the keys to my rental were still in there. A man could never be too careful.

"Then stop asking stuff that you know will get you hung up on."

She sighed, did that little sucking sound through her teeth. Gabby turned the water on in the bathroom; I could hear her humming to herself.

"I just wanted to call you and tell you about my promotion since you asked me to," Ricki said.

"I know what I asked you."

"Okay. When will you be back?"

"Monday."

"Will I see you?"

"If I'm in the mood."

She was silent for a moment. Gabby walked out of the bathroom toward the bed, then stopped to look at me. There was a smile on her face and a challenge in her eyes. She was hard to read. Asked a lot of questions, but shut down when I asked her the same questions in return. I didn't really think we needed the twenty-one question game anyway. Figured she was only using them to make up her mind about having a one-night stand. I couldn't say I blamed her. She didn't come across as a woman who had sex with every random man she met.

"You're mad at me now, aren't you?" Ricki asked.

"No, I'm not."

"We normally see each other on Mondays."

"I'm normally not coming back from a business trip either," I said as I pulled my pants on.

I held the phone between my ear and shoulder as I adjusted my belt, then buckled it.

"Okay. I know I shouldn't have said I missed you or asked about who you were with. I know your rules. I don't do this all the time."

"Yeah, but you do it enough to where I can remember each time you have done it."

"I won't do it again."

I hated when she did this shit. Hated when she got into her emotions and started to push them off on me. I hated when her feelings were hurt because she made me start to feel like the asshole I knew I was. During the three years we'd been doing this, I could count on one hand the times she'd lost herself and tried to show her emotional attachment. Each time it had been easy to make her remember why I kept her around. As long as she kept to the rules, she'd be okay.

"I know. Just like the first five times, right?" I finally answered her. "I'll call you back."

Ricki didn't say anything. She just hung up the phone. I shook my head, then clipped my phone to the case on my hip.

"The only way I'm going to have a problem with you being on the phone with another woman in my presence is if that was your wife," Gabby said. "Not that I have a right to say anything, anyway, but I don't want to be helping a married man cheat on his wife."

I cast a glance in her direction, gave a lazy smile, then quirked a brow. "Thought we had this discussion already."

"We did," she said as she pulled the gown over her head.

I couldn't help the fact that my eyes mapped her body. Everything was right where it was supposed to be. At close to forty, she put a lot of younger women's bodies to shame. I had a thing for slim women with toned waists and thick behinds, especially if they were dark skinned with natural hair. Gabby's thighs held a gap that made my mouth water.

"I told you I'm not married. I have no woman. No girlfriend. Not that it would matter at this point if I did anyway because you've already done the deed," I said, then chuckled.

"Touché."

She studied me for a moment, head tilted to the side. She stood there like she wasn't ass naked. Like it meant nothing that I drank in the sight of her as if I was parched.

"You smile a lot, but it never reaches your eyes. Do you know that?" she asked.

I turned my lips down and shrugged. "Never thought about it."

"You're smiling, but your eyes say something different."

"So you're a doctor of the mind now? Thought you were into sports medicine."

She laughed. It coated my insides. Traveled down to my stomach and settled in my dick. It jumped against my will.

"I can read people better than most of those head shrinks. Just trying to figure out the man behind the façade. You come off like you have it all figured out, but I watch people. And you have a lot more beneath the surface."

I didn't know how much I liked the fact that she was trying to read me. Didn't see why it was so important to her one way or the other. After this was all said and done, I would move on, and so would she. I was surprised when she closed the gap between us. I chuckled. I knew she was short, but seeing her out of heels proved just how much shorter than me she really was. With her hands on her minimal hips, she gazed up at me. Ran her hand up my abs like I belonged to her.

"What you see is what you get," I told her.

"That's a lie."

"Why do you care? Last night will be all we had."

"Either you're telling me my sex was trash, or you're saying that if I invited you back here tonight you wouldn't accept."

I thumbed my nose, then reached out to massage her perfect breasts. I'd never been a fan of big breasts. I didn't need all those D cups overflowing.

"I can assure you, your sex wasn't trash."

"So then you're saying tonight you won't be coming back," she said more as a statement than a question.

"Are you asking me to?"

I tugged at her locs. Sat down on the ottoman behind me so I could have better leverage. I knew I should have been on my way back to Hilton Head since I had to be back on Tybee by noon, but what man would have been able to turn down temptation ripe for the picking? I sucked her right nipple into my mouth while my hands found her small waist. Something about the way a woman rubbed my head and ears always got to me. Most women didn't know those two things increased my arousal.

I released a low growl while I palmed her ass. Her moans and hisses worked my nerve endings. Had me rising to the occasion again when all I'd intended to do was get up and leave. I lifted her up so she could straddle my lap, my mouth never leaving her breasts while she worked my belt buckle. Thankfully, the condoms were within reach behind me on the dresser. I reached back and grabbed one and gave it to her. My eyes rolled in the back of my head a bit when she massaged my head with her fingers. While I kissed on her breasts, I let my tongue travel up to her neck and ears.

Gabby was stroking me with her hand. I could feel my preexcitement leak out. She was moving her hips like she was already riding me. But I remembered how uncomfortable my length and girth had been for her last night. So I moved one hand from her locs, then slipped two fingers inside of her and stroked her with that *come here* motion to get her juices flowing again. She was already so wet. Like she had been thinking about fucking me the whole time.

She threw her head back and moaned . . . sighed like my fingers were what she had been waiting for. She rocked her hips against my hand while our breathing synchronized.

"You should come back tonight," she whispered heatedly.

"Put the condom on," I answered.

She did. Took my dick in her hand, then guided me into her. Gabby took her time. Took me in at her pace. Took the time to get adjusted, then started to move her body like a snake. She was going so painfully slow that my hand fisted the skin on her back. Yeah, she knew what she was doing. And while I may have been in control last night, this morning, she was proving that she could give as good as she can take.

I waited in the car for Carl. After Gabby and I had done our final dance of carnal pleasure, I got dressed. She headed to the shower. Neither one of us pretended to be more than what we were to each other, which was two grownups who had provided each other with sexual satisfaction. That was all there was to it.

I watched as Carl paused, then toss something in the trash as he walked out the front door. Shell locked the door behind him. She waved at me through the closed glass door, then rushed back up the stairs. Carl casually strolled out the front door like he hadn't just helped a woman to cheat on her husband. His locs swung around his shoulders. His shirt was wrinkled and untucked, and his suit jacket was in his hand while he texted on his cell.

"You look pissed," I said to him once he got into the car. "Pussy that bad?"

He shook his head. "Nah. Dalisay texting me with her bullshit."

"You still talking to her?"

"She's still my wife, and unfortunately, she's trying to contest this divorce."

I nodded and took one last look at the beach house, remembering the woman inside before I pulled off.

"How did things go with you and Shell?" I asked him.

"She's cool. Feeling her out. What about you and her friend?"

"Just good sex."

"Nothing else, huh?"

I glanced at him before putting my eyes back on the road. "Nope. Wasn't looking for there to be."

Carl chuckled, then let his seat back. I drove the rest of the way to Hilton Head in silence.

Chapter 12

Carl

It was a quiet ride back to Hilton Head, South Carolina. Diego didn't say anything more on the eighty-minute drive because he was being his usual elusive self; nothing new when it came to women. I had a feeling Shell's friend would end up being yet another casualty in a long line of what I called "hit-it-and-quit-it chicks." My friend was famous for meeting a woman, sexing her, and cutting her off at the drop of a hat, especially if she seemed to start catching feelings. This had been a pattern with Diego throughout all the years I'd known him; he always kept women at arm's length, and when they seemed to get too close, *poof*, they were gone like yesterday's trash.

I guess that's why the arrangement between Diego and his old standby, Ricki, had worked out so well for him; he was in complete control. Ricki was young; young enough, in fact, to be Diego's daughter. And he had her trained like a child. Or better yet, a puppy. He said jump and didn't have to say how high because she already knew. At times, I actually felt sorry for her, because although Diego was my best friend, ole boy was clearly taking advantage of her. I wanted to chalk it up to her being young and dumb, but then again, he was breaking her off with money and other gifts. Maybe the situation worked for her too.

Ricki's dilemma made me think of the young lady that I recently shared a bed with. Shell also appeared to be in a situation that she had no control over; a cheating husband who had apparently moved on with another woman, and yet she had no means to escape the marriage. Yeah, she had a temporary furlough for the weekend, but from what I gathered, that motherfucker could potentially make her life a living hell once she got back.

During the silence on the ride to Hilton Head, I thought back to the few minutes I spent with Shell before Diego and I left.

Shell was asleep wearing nothing but an Atlanta Falcons football jersey. I hadn't been with another woman in almost twenty years, seventeen of those married. But now that I no longer considered myself married, all bets were off. I had to admit, I didn't feel one ounce of guilt whatsoever over what happened with Shell. Betrayal will do that to you. And the fact that that was some good-ass pussy made it all the better. Tight, juicy, sweet. Damn. My mouth was watering just from thinking about it.

I'm a man who's used to getting what I want, and I wanted another taste of Shell. Even though she was asleep, I didn't think she would mind if I helped myself. I moved closer to her, sliding my hand between her legs, gently massaging her clit. She began to moan softly, her legs parting as if inviting me in. One finger entered her moist folds, while my thumb continued to stimulate her clit. I saw her briefly open her eyes, then close them again as they rolled back in her head.

I only had about an hour's sleep, and I needed a pick-me-up. Usually that was coffee, but Shell's juicy pussy would work just fine. Sliding my head between her legs, my tongue teased her clit.

"What are you doing to me, Carl?"

I grabbed her meaty thighs, placing them on my shoulders. My tongue found its way into her sweet, pink pussy as I tongue fucked her, my nose rubbing up against her sensitive clit.

As I moved my tongue and face in concentric circles, Shell let me know how much she appreciated my attention.

"Damn, Carl, that shit feels so good," she said, as she moved to match my movements. "Suck my pussy."

I loved it when a woman knew what she wanted and wasn't afraid to say so. I grabbed her waist, my face burying even deeper. Her legs began to shake while she held my head in place. For a minute, I felt as if I was going to suffocate. Fuck it. If I died right then and there, at least I'd die happy. Besides, wouldn't that be a bitch if Dalisay got a call from the cops telling her how I died? "Ma'am, your husband died with his head between another woman's legs." It'd be poetic justice if you asked me.

"Oh shit, oh shit, Oh Shit!" Shell repeated, her juices squirting all over my face. I drank her sweet come until it was all gone.

"Good morning," I said, lifting my head up. All she could do was laugh.

I took my glasses off, wiped my hand down my face, and noticed Shell's essence was still on my fingers. I smiled to myself. Hadn't done that in weeks, smiled, that is. Maybe a fake one for staff, clients, and other business associates, but not a real, genuine smile. Being with Shell did that. Like I said earlier, misery does indeed love company, and that misery tasted *really* good.

My reminiscing was interrupted by the continuous vibration of my phone. Checking it, I saw it was Dali. The bitch was really beginning to work my nerves. I thought about ignoring the call, but I knew if I didn't answer, she'd keep calling back.

"What?" I asked, wanting her to know how annoyed I truly was.

"I've been trying to reach you all morning. Why haven't you answered my text messages?"

"Because there was no need."

"What do you mean there was no need? I tell you I'm contesting the divorce, and you ignore me?"

"And I'm supposed to care why?"

Although it just started, I was already tired of this conversation.

"Because, Carl, I still love you. I think we can work through this."

What the fuck? This woman was obviously delusional. That or her pregnancy hormones were seriously fucking with her brain. "Are you out of your goddamn mind? You didn't love me when you were boning the fuck out of John. Not to mention you're in the family way, except—wait, it's not *our* family. Bitch, please! Get the fuck outta here! This conversation is over. From now on, anything you want to say to me about the divorce, you can say through my lawyer."

And just that quickly, Dali killed my buzz.

"Carl, are you saying you feel nothing for me, that you don't love me at all anymore?"

I could hear the quiver in her voice, as if she was about to cry.

"Oh, I feel something for you, but it definitely is *not* love. You might want to stop asking questions like that or I might tell you what it is I *really* feel for you."

Diego was pulling into the parking lot of the Omni Hilton Head Oceanfront Resort. Aside from the occasional sniffle, I heard crickets on the other end of the phone. Finally, she spoke.

"I know you're angry, and you have every right to be, but please, please, just think about it. That's all I ask."

Ain't this some shit! This bitch was thickheaded as fuck! She cheated, she rawdogged, she got knocked up with someone else's baby—What part of all that was I supposed to forgive? Hell no! Not happening!

"Dali, I have to go. Business to attend to."

"Okay, Carl. Just remember, I still love—" I quickly disconnected the call.

"You okay, man?" Diego asked as we exited our vehicle.

"Yeah, I'm good."

"You sure? Because if you're not, I can handle the meeting today."

I knew Diego was just as tired as I was, so I wasn't going to leave him to handle things on his own. Besides, I wasn't one to slack off when it came to business, no matter what I was dealing with personally. In reality, until last night, work was my only distraction. Now I had another, at least for this weekend.

"Bro, you know me; I need to keep busy. Going to the meeting and going to the fair are just what I need to get my mind off of my issues. Understand?"

We quickly walked through the lobby, heading toward the elevator.

"Yeah, I hear you. But if you feel the need to take a break, just let me know."

"Thanks, man," I said, entering the elevator, pressing the button for the top floor.

Diego and I both had luxury oceanfront suites. After one particularly bothersome incident when Diego and I were in college, I always knew to get my own room when we traveled anywhere. We had gotten a two-bedroom suite, and even though my room was across the hall, I was stuck hearing some random female he met in a club screaming, "Aye, papi," all fucking night long. Needless to say, that was the first *and* last time we shared a room, because I never knew if Diego was going to end up with a flavor of the night.

The elevator doors slid open, and Diego and I parted ways, heading to our respective rooms. The plan was to rendezvous at eight thirty at HH Prime, one of the hotel's upscale restaurants, for breakfast, as well as a quick strategy session, before heading to the conference room we rented in order to interview several companies vying to handle marketing for Electron Enterprises. We already had a kick-ass marketing team, but we knew that if we wanted to stay current, we needed fresh, new ideas, and getting other opinions never hurt.

Before entering my room, I looked at my watch and saw that it was seven thirty. I needed to get a move on. I was starting to feel the effects of my night out. My eyelids felt heavy, and my eyes started to burn. I let out a hearty yawn. Walking over to the suite's mini kitchen, I grabbed a coffee mug, opened a packet of the hotel's instant fresh roast coffee, and poured it into the cup. Time was passing, so instead of waiting for the coffeemaker to heat some water, I put some water from the sink in the mug, and then placed the cup in the microwave, setting the time for one minute thirty seconds.

While my coffee was heating up, I got out some clothes to wear. I chose a pair of charcoal-gray pants, matching socks, a crisp light gray Polo shirt, and my black leather oxfords. Even the boxer briefs I selected were gray, the color reflecting my current mood thanks to my hopefully soon-to-be ex-wife. She really had me fucked up. How could she even have the nerve to contest the divorce? She didn't have a leg to stand on. I clearly had the tramp on the grounds of adultery. The DNA test proved that. Yeah, she was trippin'. The more I thought about her, the more disgusted I became.

I was jolted out of my thoughts when I heard the microwave ring. I opened the door, taking the cup with the steaming hot coffee out. I didn't even wait for it to cool down. I damn near burned my taste buds off drinking the strong liquid. I needed it strong right now. I saw many cups in my future this morning; didn't want to fall asleep during the interviews.

I made short work of the cup, and then headed to the shower, took off my glasses placing them, along with my cell phone, on the bathroom counter. Quickly, I shed my clothes, tossed them to the side. Turning on the water, I gave it a few seconds to warm up. I needed a hot shower; did some of my best thinking then.

I stepped inside, turned around, letting the hot water roll down my back. As I inhaled the steam, I allowed myself to relax a bit. Before I left Shell, we talked for a few minutes. You can learn a lot about a person in a short amount of time if you really wanted to. And I wanted to know more about the woman I had been sexing for the better part of the night.

"What are you going to school for?" I asked as I got dressed.

Shell was lying on her stomach; head sitting on her hands, Falcons jersey half covering her full bare ass. I had to look away, or else I'd never get out of there.

"I'm prelaw. I eventually want to study international law."

I almost tuned her out when she said she wanted to become a lawyer, but I had to remember that it wasn't her fault that she wanted to go into the same profession as Dalisay. That was just my own transference talking.

"Why international law?"

She tilted her head to the side and took a deep breath as she appeared to be formulating an answer.

"I love studying the law, and I want to travel. That way, I have the best of both worlds."

I didn't want to burst her bubble, but one question kept gnawing at me.

"How are you going to travel if your husband doesn't even like you going to school locally? If you two get back together, you know that'll probably be an issue."

"Assuming we do get back together, I guess I'll cross that bridge if and when it comes to that," she shrugged. "Once I graduate, and he sees all the opportunities I'll have, I'm sure he'll change his mind."

"Well, I hope it all works out for you." I felt Shell was being extremely naïve, but if that's what it took to get her through the day, then so be it. "How old are your kids?" I asked.

"I have a girl who is three, and a boy who is four."

I put on my shoes and glasses, picked up my cell.

"Think you'll have anymore?"

"Most likely. I do love children. But that won't be any time soon. Not until I graduate and have a decent job." Shell got up from the bed. "Do you have any kids?"

I bristled when I heard her question.

"No. Wife didn't want any. Was too concerned with climbing the corporate ladder."

As I considered the bitter irony, the subject still had me feeling raw.

The look on Shell's face told me she also understood how ironic the situation was. "Damn, Carl, that's really fucked up."

"It is what it is."

At the moment, my phone vibrated in my hand. I thought it may have been Diego sending me a text letting me know he was ready to go. Instead, Dali's name popped up. Just one of a number of text messages. All of them pissed me off, all of them went unanswered. I rolled my eyes, putting my phone in my back pocket.

Shell noticed the look of aggravation on my face.

"Something wrong?"

Didn't feel like getting into it, so I flat-out lied. "No. Just business. Give me your phone."

"Why?" she questioned.

"Just give it to me."

Reluctantly, she complied before stepping into the bathroom. Going to her contacts, I pressed the icon for a new entry. I entered my information and saved it. Then I dialed my number. I let it go to voice mail. I just needed her number to show up in the call log so I could lock it in my phone. Shell returned wearing a pair of shorts. I handed the phone back to her. "Last night was . . . good," I said, walking toward the front door.

"So was this morning," she laughed.

I watched her ass jiggle as she paraded in front of me, unlocking the front door. I tapped her on it, making her jump. I wanted to tap it again . . . in more ways than one.

"You ladies have a good time at the fair today."

"Thank you," she replied. "And, Carl."

"Yes?" I asked as I walked out the door.

"Thank you. For everything else." A huge grin crossed her face.

"You're welcome," I said.

Then I thought to myself, Yeah, my time with Shell isn't over yet. Not by a long shot.

I got out of the shower, dried off, and quickly got dressed. When I arrived at the restaurant at eight thirty on the dot, Diego was already there. He had gotten us a table with a clear view of the ocean. He had also gotten us a large pot of coffee.

"Wasn't sure you were going to make it," he chuckled. "I guess Shell really worked you over last night."

"Very funny, motherfucker. You got jokes," I said, pouring a cup of coffee. "The coffee's half gone, so I'm guessing it's safe to say you didn't get much sleep either."

Diego took a sip of the light colored beverage. His idea of coffee was more like a whole bunch of sugar and milk with just a touch of coffee.

"True. So you want to talk about what happened with Dalisay?"

"You heard what happened."

"No, I heard what you *said* to her. I don't want to make assumptions about what's really going on."

He looked me squarely in the eyes. In a way, I felt I owed Diego the truth when it came to Dalisay. If it wasn't for him, I might be in prison for assault . . . or worse, and even though she was the one who called him, I know he was looking out for me, not her.

"She doesn't want a divorce. Claims we can work it out."

Diego had a look of surprise on his face.

"You can't tell me she really believes that. I mean, after *everything* she did, she can't possibly think you'd take her back."

"Apparently she does," I replied.

Our food arrived. I tore into it like it was my last meal.

"For what it's worth, I think you're doing the right thing. Let the lawyers handle it. See, this is just one more reason why I don't want to get married," he said.

"Negro, please, stop making excuses for why you don't want to get married. You just like playing the field," I retorted, laughing. "Although, if you ask me, Ricki's the closest thing you've had to a girlfriend in a minute."

"You're right," Diego sneered, looking up from his meal. "Nobody asked you."

I hardly ever brought up Ricki, but Diego had that young woman around for so long, I wasn't lying when I said she was the closest thing he had to a girlfriend. I felt if your best friend couldn't tell you the truth, then who could?

"Be an asshole if you want, but that girl is going to expect more from you, probably sooner rather than later, and you're going to be left with two choices: either man up, or let her go."

Diego huffed. "Ricki knows better than to even try to give me an ultimatum. She knows what will happen if she does," he replied, smugness in his tone.

"Okay, bro, if you say so. Just don't let those words come back to bite you in the ass," I said.

"Never gonna happen," he chortled, haughtiness oozing from those words.

I looked at him, shaking my head.

"All right, man. I hope you're right. But when she goes all *Fatal Attraction* on you, don't come crying to me. Just remember, little girls who get their feelings hurt can eventually become scornful, bitter women, and there's no telling what she might do then. On that note, I'm done."

I let it go because I knew talking to Diego sometimes was like talking to a brick wall; it got you nowhere.

"'Bout damn time," he laughed. "Look, man, I appreciate what you're saying, but I know Ricki a lot better than you do, and I know she won't make waves, and she's not going anywhere, so it's all good. Now, let's talk business."

Now that was something Diego and I could always agree on. The rest of our breakfast time was spent brainstorming, and while it was productive, my mind was elsewhere, mainly on my looming divorce that was about to become very messy. I just couldn't shake the feeling that my life was about to get a lot more complicated.

Chapter 13

Mischelle

The smell of bacon greeted me once I finally opened my eyes. I jumped up from my sleep with a slow drum of satisfaction beating between my thighs. My phone was beeping from my clutch across the room, and I remembered all that had happened before Carl had left this morning. It came rushing back like a 3-D movie. Oh God, what had I done?

I'd really cheated on Malik. I'd broken my vows. I didn't know how to feel about that. Even though Malik had been a grade-A asshole and had cheated on me, I questioned my moral standings because I'd turned around and done the same thing to him. Jesus, what had I done? Had I been so drunk in lust that I'd lost my mind?

Possibly so. But the way Carl had handled me sent chills up my spine. The way he'd explored my body like he'd been specifically sent to do it made me close my eyes and shutter. I could feel my breasts swelling and nipples hardening at the thought of it. To see his beautifully handsome face between my thighs before he left had stunned me. And my, oh my, could that man eat some pussy. The way his thick tongue would flatten against my lips just before he would lick from my opening up to my clit had me on edge. My stomach clenched involuntarily as I got the sensation all over again.

I sat up. Felt my body aching as if I had worked out with one of those CrossFit training freaks. My inner thighs were sore from where Carl's big hands had spread my thighs while he worked his hips against my pelvis. He could move his hips like no man I'd ever encountered. Carl wasn't afraid of hip thrusting and whining. He'd shown me that on the dance floor. I shouldn't have been surprised that he wouldn't mind doing the same in bed.

I yawned as I stood. Scratched my fat ass as I walked over to the dresser to take my phone from my clutch. I could still taste the stale alcohol on my breath, and it made me frown. The hardwood floor was cold underneath my feet. I saw I had missed calls from Malik and guilt settled into the pit of my stomach like anvils. Walking over to the window, I closed it as it was a bit chilly in the room. Then I dialed my husband's cell and waited for him to answer.

"Why you ain't answer your phone?" Malik asked as soon as he picked up the phone.

"I was sleeping," I stated flatly.

"What were you doing last night that has you sleeping the day through?"

I almost stuttered when I opened my mouth. Started to chew on my bottom lip. Three golden condom wrappers lay haphazardly on the floor while Carl's scent saturated my skin. He smelled so good, the scent he'd worn was like an aphrodisiac. I kept seeing his face as his locs swung around his shoulders and back that morning. He'd taken his locs down after the first time we'd sexed. They were a lot longer than they looked in the braids. They sat middle of his back.

Malik had always been good at reading me, and the last thing I needed was for him to call me on my shit before I could think of a plausible excuse. Yes, he'd cheated on me, but did I need him to know what I had been doing?

No.

I told him, "Gabby and I went out last night."

"So you staying out all night like a filthy ho just because you ain't at home? You left my kids somewhere just to go clubbing?"

I sighed heavily. "You got some damn nerve," I spat out venomously. "Some fucking nerve when you're the one who ran off and left your whole damn family for some piece of young ass."

"I didn't run off and leave my family. I left *you*," he shot back coolly.

His words stung. I couldn't pretend they didn't. I had to swallow my pride and tears. The bile that had risen in my throat threatened to come up.

Malik didn't seem to care that his words cut like the sharpest two-edged sword. He kept right at it. "So get that shit straight, I left you. I left a woman who put her little book writing shit and school before her husband. Left a woman who wouldn't give her husband no pussy. Found somebody who actually paid attention to me."

The tears that I'd been fighting against started to stroll down my cheeks.

"So you want a divorce is what you're saying?" I asked him, just for clarity.

"I don't want to be with you no more. I don't."

I inhaled and exhaled heavily. "Malik, this is a marriage. You don't just walk away from a marriage. This isn't some rinky-dink relationship. We stood before God and took vows!"

"Yo, where my kids?" he asked, completely ignoring everything I'd just said.

"Malik!"

"Where my kids?"

Outside my window, it was cloudy, but had just enough sunlight to brighten the day for the outdoor activities of the festival. I wished I could see just a little of the sun in my life . . . in my future. As of now, gloom had settled in.

"So, you're for real? You're just going to walk out on me like that? Make me a freaking single mother because you want to chase ass?"

"Making you a single mother because you chose to be one. You had a husband, but I guess other shit was more important than me."

"Malik, I stay at home all the damn time," I explained, tears rushing down my cheeks. "I go to Washington once a year for a book conference. I go to school at home for the most part! I work from home! What more do you want from me?"

Malik barked into the phone. "Pay attention to a nigga sometimes. You stay shut up in that damn room doing whatever it is you do on the computer. I come home from work and have to take the kids. Shit, I get tired too. Then you won't give a nigga no pussy. I can't even get my dick handled because you put your work and your school before me."

"Malik, all I asked from you was to watch the kids for a few hours after work so I can get some work done. That's it. You're barely getting any hours at work. So I work extra hard to meet deadlines so I can get advances. Work damn hard to keep my GPA up so I can qualify for scholarships so what's left can be sent back to me so I can help with bills around the house. You don't want me to work outside the home. You don't want me to go anywhere," I yelled. "Jesus Christ, what *else* do you want from me!"

I knew he could hear me crying. By now, I couldn't stop the tears from falling. The soul wracking sobs shook my shoulders and weakened me to the point I plopped down on the bed behind me.

"I don't want to hear all that shit. Where the fuck my kids at? Your moms got them or what?" was all he said to me.

When all I could do was cry, not giving him the answer he wanted, he hung up on me. I dropped the phone on the bed wondering what had I done to him to make him treat me like I meant nothing to him. I wracked my brain trying to remember a time when I had made my husband feel less than. I went out of my way to never disrespect the man. Did everything he asked me to, and it still wasn't enough.

I showered in solemnness. Tried to wash away the memories of Carl and couldn't. Tried to lather up enough soap to get rid of the sin I'd committed. Not only was I married, but Carl was too, no matter if he was going through a divorce. My God, what I was thinking? As I beat myself up, I pulled on a pair of yoga pants and a tank for the time being and headed downstairs. My braids hung down my back.

Gabby had the sliding door open, leaving the screen closed. For the life of me, I didn't want to burden her with my woes so I fixed myself up best I could. As the waves hugged the shore for the moment, the call of the seagulls and other birds could still be heard. The sizzling of frying bacon greeted me. Scrambled eggs sat fluffy on a serving tray along with golden toast.

"Well, it's nice of you to join the living," Gabby jibed once she realized I was in the kitchen.

I smiled and headed for the pitcher of orange juice. She was smiling, but I could see that she was tired. Dressed in only red biking shorts and a sports bra, I could tell she was relaxed.

I poured myself some juice and said, "Ugh. I barely got any sleep," I told her.

"I heard," she said, then laughed.

I rolled my eyes, a bit embarrassed at it all. Still, when those memories came flashing back, I had to grab ahold of the counter.

"I feel so bad, Gabby," I told her.

She didn't ask about what. She knew exactly what I was talking about because she knew me.

She rolled her eyes. "The deed is done now, Shell. Can't take it back, so there is no need to beat yourself up over it. Did you at least enjoy it?"

I nodded as a slow smile adorned my features. "I did. Best sex I've had in a long time. I'm not sure how to feel now. On one hand, I enjoyed myself a little too much, and on the other hand, I feel like crap because I betrayed my vows."

"Girl, Malik has been betraying those vows since I've known you."

"Yeah, but—"

"But what?"

She gave me a side eye as she stirred grits on the stove. I hadn't expected her to be cooking grits. She hated the things. Thought they were disgusting. So there was no doubt she was cooking them for me.

"You'd better not be about to stand up here and say anything that remotely sounds as if you're about to excuse Malik's behavior. I heard you upstairs, so I know what happened. Screw him. Let's not forget that bacterial vaginosis you had almost two years ago. And I'm not here to beat you over the head with I told you so, but I *did* tell you so."

I thought back to the time when I'd thought Malik may have given me an STI. After jumping down his throat, only to have him deny it vehemently, I had called Gabby in a panic because my vagina smelled like a fish had crawled inside of me and died. Most traumatic moment in my personal life. Luckily, my doctor had told me that BV didn't necessarily have to come from sexual inter-course. She'd told me it could have come from a number of things that may have caused my vaginal pH balance to become unbalanced. So I chalked it up to that and left it alone. Now it was coming back to haunt me.

Gabby turned to look at me.

With a hand on her waist she said, "Shell, I can explain it to you, but I can't understand it for you. Malik has done you a favor. And I'll just leave that right there. Now back to you and Carl. Did he treat you like a cheap whore and leave money on the nightstand?"

As much as I wanted to be mad at her for saying how she felt—making me feel stupid in the process—I couldn't help but laugh at what she'd asked.

"No, but I wish he would have. Checked my bank account this morning and it's not happening for me."

Gabby waved her hand. "Give me your account number again and I'll transfer you some money over."

I started shaking my head. "Gabby, no. You've already done enough. I have debt with you now. I know you're trying to help, but no. I'm just venting, I promise. Just because I talk about my issues, I don't want you to think I'm fishing for money."

Gabby frowned, went to the sink to fill a glass with water, then tossed it on me.

A big splash of water hit my face, neck, ears, and chest. I squealed and inhaled hard. I couldn't believe she had done that.

"Gabby, what the hell?" I yelled.

"That's for insulting me, and because I know if I hit you I'm too tired to fight your country thick behind off me. I would never in my life think you were fishing for money because you vented your problems to me! What the heck kind of friend would I be if I thought such a thing? Who does that?" she quipped, a bit angrily.

"I wasn't trying to offend you. I just wanted you to know that—"

"I don't care. You *did* offend me. I'm your friend, and if the first thing I think is that you're fishing for money when you come to me, then I don't know how to be a true friend."

With that, she walked off and headed to the bathroom. I rushed over to grab the grits so they wouldn't burn. She'd made me feel bad about the whole thing. I hadn't meant any harm. Just wanted her to know that as my friend she wasn't obligated to help me and that I would never abuse her generosity as such.

I guess just because I didn't mean any harm doesn't mean I didn't cause any. When she came out of the bathroom, I apologized to her. She accepted. We hugged it out and moved on. I walked over to the door and looked out. The scenery looked as if it should have been put on a postcard. Even though the air was a little cool and the sun was battling the clouds for dominance, the beauty of the island couldn't be denied.

"I can't believe I had sex with a man I'd met only hours before," I said after a while, talking to myself more so than Gabby.

"I can't either, but, hey, it happens all the time."

"Yeah, but not with me."

She shrugged. "First time for everything."

My brows furrowed, and I walked over to feel her head to see if she had a fever.

She knocked my hand away from her head and asked, "What?"

"Trying to see if you have a fever. Is this the same Gabby from last night? The one who was trying to talk me out of a one-night stand?"

She shook her head and rolled her eyes as she put the last of the bacon on the serving tray.

"Oh my gosh," I yelled. "You slept with Diego, *didn't* you?" I asked.

She tried to hide a smile as she picked up the tray and went to set it on the circular glass dining table. I grabbed the juice and two glasses since she had already set the table. She took a seat. Once the food was blessed, I kept staring at her.

"What, Shell?"

"Are you going to tell me if it was even good or not?"

She chuckled. "I didn't say I did anything!"

"But you did. I *know* you did."

"How?"

"Because if you hadn't, you would be scolding me right now."

"I mean, you're grown, so you can do what you want."

"Which is apparently what *you* did."

She took a bite of her bacon, and then looked back up at me. "Yes, I did, and no, I don't regret it. I thought I would, but I don't. It was fun actually, and it was worth it."

I couldn't believe it. The woman who was against one-night stands had participated in one. Then again, I'd done the same. So there we were, two peas in a pod. Of course, I needed to know if he was as good in bed as he looked. *Had* to know. Diego was fine as shit and being as tall as he was, I had to wonder if he was well equipped.

"So is he one of those brothers whose height and good looks makes up for the fact he has a little dick?" I asked.

"No, I must say, he is *very* well taken care of in the penis department. Took me a minute to adjust to the size."

I grinned wide. It had been so long since she'd had some good dick. I knew it was crass, but I didn't understand her pain until my husband had started to drop the ball sexually in our marriage. It really sucked not to be getting good sex, but it sucked more when you had available dick, and they still couldn't satisfy you. So I would never be mad at her for taking the bull by the horns and riding that motherfucker until the hooves fell off.

We laughed and talked some more, then cleaned up the kitchen as we talked about the night before. Afterward, we took some time to pick out outfits for the day. She chose black tights that looked as if they had been painted on, a cute turquoise baby doll top with high-top sneakers of the same colors. I thought the simple attire looked absolutely gorgeous on her. Showed off her shape and brought out the youthful features she had.

I decided to be daring. I grabbed a pair denim shorts to go over my black leggings. I hadn't worn shorts in years, and I knew if Malik had seen me in them he would have a fit. But as I slid them over my thighs and hips, I couldn't help but enjoy the freedom this weekend had allotted me. I pulled on a fish tail button-down shirt. The fish tail just meant it was longer in the back than in the front. I had on black combat boots that came up to my knees.

I pulled my braids into a ponytail, then went to help Gabby style her locs. The woman had a lot of healthy hair, and I often wondered how she handled it when I wasn't around. Anytime she and I got together, she said she would breathe a sigh of relief that I could help her do her locs. Not that she couldn't, it was just that I knew an array of styles she could wear and often styled her hair in many of them.

Once we were all fancied up and ready to go, we headed out. I was glad it hadn't started to rain again. I really wanted to get out and enjoy the day. The drive to town wasn't really much of a drive at all. The streets were blocked off so you had to pay for parking and walk the rest of the way to whichever event you wanted to take in. There was a big DJ booth set up at the end of the street and a makeshift dance floor that already seemed to be crowded. Grills were going at every corner. Food trucks sat about. You could smell different kinds of food for miles. Arts and crafts were on display, as well as hand sewn clothing being sold by different African American designers. The weather didn't seem to be on anyone's mind.

"So, you plan on seeing Carl again before you leave?" Gabby asked me once we had parked the car.

We passed through the sea of people crowding the street. I looked up at the big banner advertising the twenty-fifth annual celebration for the black community in Savannah and the year's theme was "Dare to Dream; Create a Legacy." Gabby had wanted to catch the play *Flyin' West*. As the day went on, she and I found ourselves in the thick of things. If you didn't know, Savannah had a rich African American history. Gabby and I were trying to keep cognizant of the time since at seven that evening we were supposed to head to the Savannah State University's Kennedy Fine Arts Building to see *Flyin' West*.

The play was set in Nicodemus, Kansas, in 1898, and depicts the story of courageous, black pioneer women, former slaves, and free women of color, who went west to build a new life for themselves. Gabby was all for women's empowerment and loved things that showed how we as black women overcame such a tumultuous time.

I wanted to catch the W. W. Law Lecture Series, named after Westley Wallace Law who was born in the 1920s and was one of the most prominent civil rights leaders in Savannah. So we started to walk toward the Savannah Civic Center. We had our whole day mapped out.

I shook my head. "I don't think I can do that again. I just can't. I'm barely able to live with myself now. As good as he was in bed, I'm good on that. What about you? You thinking about getting some of Diego again?"

She smiled. "I did tell Diego he was invited if he wanted to come back."

My eyes widened. "What?"

"Hey, don't judge me. It's been a minute. And besides, who says a woman can't enjoy a little responsible fun?"

"Errr . . . you. *You* told me that."

"Do as I say, darn it, not as I do!" she said with a laugh.

I playfully shoved her. "You're so full of it."

Chapter 14

Gabrielle

Shell and I walked around checking out the various booths that lined the streets. The temperature had warmed up nicely, despite the looming clouds. While it appeared to be the calm before the storm, the threat of rain didn't deter the throngs of revelers. Although the event was designed to celebrate the rich heritage of black Americans, people from all backgrounds partook in the numerous festivities. Good food, good drink, and good music all seemed to have a way of bringing people together.

Generally, I'm a very healthy person, but this was my weekend to indulge. I was dying for something sweet and came across a shop located on East River Street. Savannah's Candy Kitchen had just what I needed to fill my craving. I dragged Shell inside, much to her dismay.

"Gabby, why do I have to go in there with you? I'll probably gain ten pounds just *looking* at all that stuff," she protested.

Sighing, I said, "Ma'am, if it makes you feel any better, you can wait outside." I knew how sensitive she was about her weight.

She quickly bolted for the door, leaving me standing there with my mouth open. As I surveyed the shop, I noticed the wide assortment of confections; an assortment of pralines, taffies, turtles, baked goods, fudges, and numerous other sweets filled the place. I needed to pick something quickly before I went overboard. I settled on a quarter pound of maple walnut fudge, then made my way back to Shell.

She was at a booth that sold scented oils. I had a weakness for those; owned quite a few. I loved them because not only could they be used as body fragrances; they also could be used in oil warmers at home. I picked out a few for myself, as well as for Shell, paying the vendor.

"Damn, Gabby."

"What?" I was taken aback by her reaction.

"You have to stop spending your money on me. You make me feel like a pauper because I can't really afford anything."

My brow furrowed in confusion. "It's just a few bottles of scented oil. What's the big deal?"

"The big deal is I couldn't even afford to buy them for myself."

While I understood why she felt the way she did as far as her money situation was concerned, what I couldn't understand was why, after we'd had been friends for so long, she would still have issues with me doing little things like this. Sometimes she was just too prideful. But I wasn't going to belabor the point.

"Fine, if that's how you feel, I won't buy you anything else."

"Look, Gabby, I don't want you to think I'm ungrateful; it's just that I hate that I can't get the things I want. And I hate feeling like a charity case."

I looked at her. "Shell, if that's how you really feel, then that's on you. But like I said, I won't buy you anything else."

We walked in silence for a while. I didn't want to argue. I wanted to enjoy the festival, and the rest of my time on the island. Wasn't in the mood for pity parties or drama, and right now, Shell was being a real Debbie Downer.

But when we came upon a particular booth, her mood instantly changed.

It was the booth for Electron Enterprises. It appeared to be fully staffed with employees performing health assessments. There was a sizable line of festivalgoers patiently waiting to receive the various services. At the booth, handing out pamphlets and chatting with participants, were Diego and Carl. I glanced at Shell, who was trying to hide the slight smile on her face. I could tell by her body language that although she felt guilty because of what she had done, she wasn't completely guilt-ridden.

Carl was the first to notice us. He was dressed in semi-casual business attire appropriate for the occasion. He gave a nod of acknowledgment and mouthed the words, "One second."

I turned my attention to Shell. "Hmph. Looks like somebody is happy to see a certain someone," I said, crossing my arms in front of me, a smirk on my face.

"What? I . . . no . . . well . . ."

"Flustered much?" I raised an eyebrow.

Carl walked over to where we were standing. "Hello, ladies." He addressed us both, but was looking directly at Shell.

"Hey, Carl," I said, not even sure he heard me.

"Hi, Carl," Shell said, looking smitten.

Feeling like a third wheel, I excused myself to check out a booth selling African American, as well as African art. It was close enough that I could still hear and see the two of them. They were in deep conversation about the previous night's, and apparently this morning's, events. Next thing I knew, they were holding hands, and Carl, once again, had his tongue down Shell's throat. They were so blatant, an older couple commented on it.

"Young love is such a beautiful thing," the woman remarked. "Are you two married?"

Before Shell could speak, Carl responded, "Yes, we are, but not to each other."

I could have almost died. Shell looked mortified. And the looks on the older couple's faces . . . Priceless!

I focused my attention back on the artwork, still laughing to myself at what had transpired. I selected a small framed piece with a Sankofa symbol surrounding a Sankofa bird. The word *Sankofa* was derived from the Akan language from Ghana. It had been translated into several meanings, but the one I liked the most read, "We must go back and reclaim our past so we can move forward; so we understand why and how we can be who we are today." Words to live by.

As I was paying for the picture, I heard a deep voice behind me say, "Nice."

I turned around to see the towering hulk of a man that was Diego standing there, smiling down at me.

I assumed he was referring to the picture, and said as much. "I think so too. That's why I bought it."

He gave a light chuckle. "Yeah, that's nice too."

Like Carl, he too was dressed in business attire, wearing brown slacks, brown loafers, and a cream-colored long sleeve shirt that had the sleeves rolled up. Just like last night at the club, he looked like he commanded attention. That was evident by the way several women were shamelessly leering at him. One even had the nerve to wink at him with me standing right there. Although we weren't together, I was still surprised by her boldness. He ignored her. I'd never admit it out loud, but I was amused by that.

"I thought you were going to come over to the booth," he said, arms crossed in front of him. His piercing honey-colored eyes appeared to be studying me intently.

"I was, as soon as I got some shopping done. Besides, it looked pretty busy over there. I was going to wait for the crowd to die down."

He took a quick glance at the booth, still bustling with customers.

"I'm glad there's a lot of interest. Sometimes, it's hard to get people to listen."

"Tell me about it." I reflected on how, as a doctor, I became discouraged when patients didn't listen to me. "I promise I'll check it out before I leave."

"I'm going to hold you to that," he replied, as if demanding that I show up. "Am I still invited back to your place tonight?"

"If you want," I answered in a noncommittal tone.

I didn't need this man thinking I was desperate to see him again, because I wasn't. Sure, the sex was, well, awesome, but my woman's intuition was telling me that Diego was used to always getting what he wanted as far as the opposite sex was concerned. It was also telling me that he liked the chase, but once a woman stopped running, he lost interest. He was just about to comment when Shell and Carl walked up.

"The organizers are calling for an early end to the festival today. There's a big storm rolling in from a few miles away, and they don't want any issues," he remarked. "I told everyone to pack it up. Which means we're done for today." I noticed he had his arm around Shell's shoulders. "If you ladies don't have any other plans, I was thinking we could all go back to Hilton Head and have lunch."

"Actually, there's a play I wanted to see tonight, and Shell had some lectures she wanted to attend," I said.

"But we could always go tomorrow, right?" she chimed in. Giving her a look that said "Seriously?" she quickly looked away from me.

"Shell, can I speak with you for a moment?"

Without waiting for her response, I moved away from Diego and Carl. She meekly complied. She knew me well enough to know that if she didn't come with me, I would have said everything I wanted to say in front of Carl and Diego.

"What the heck? You know we had plans for today."

"Yes," she sighed, "but when Carl offered to take us to lunch back at their hotel, I just couldn't say no."

"Seriously? It's really easy. Try it with me now. *No.* Come on, your turn."

"Gabby, please," she begged. "We can always go to the lectures and the play tomorrow."

"But, Shell, this was supposed to be our weekend. We didn't come here to hook up with two random guys all weekend. As a matter of fact, we came here to get away from the men in our lives because of all the issues they were causing us. And let me remind you, Hilton Head is almost an hour away. That puts us even further from the beach house."

"I know, but I may never get this opportunity again. And I've always wanted to see the Omni from the inside. I swear, if you do this one thing for me, it'll be just you and me for the rest of the weekend."

I rubbed my hand across my forehead, then down the rest of my face. Shell was giving me a headache. I felt like she was playing on my sensitivities, knowing that I would feel sorry for her because of her home situation. Unfortunately, it was working. I hated that sometimes, I was too much of a softy.

"I don't think this is a good idea at all, for a number of reasons. Least of which is you and Carl are both married. Nothing good can come of this. But you're grown. Besides, I don't want them thinking I'm a buzz kill. We'll go, but after tonight, it's bye-bye Carl and Diego—are we clear?"

She flashed the widest grin I had ever seen her give. "Thank you, thank you, thank you." She gave me a big hug. "Tonight's it, I promise."

"Yeah, yeah," I replied, backing up a bit. "Don't make any promises, just stick to your word."

Promises meant nothing to me without action behind them. I had had too many promises made to me broken in the past to believe in them anymore. And for some reason, I felt this was going to be another one.

We walked back over to Diego and Carl. That's when I felt it; the first few drops signifying that the heavens were about to open up. With all the sinning that I assumed was about to happen, I had to wonder if the rain would be like the flood in Noah's ark.

"Everything okay?" Carl asked.

"Yes. Let's go," Shell quickly answered. Carl took her hand and interlocked her fingers with his, taking her to the place where he and Diego had parked their vehicle. They were in an area designated for vendors, which was a lot closer than where we were parked.

"Where are you parked?" Diego asked.

"About half a mile away, in the municipal parking lot."

"Hop in," Carl said. "We'll drop you off, and you can follow us from there."

I was somewhat upset with Shell, and I felt inclined to walk back by myself, but it was no longer drizzling. The rain had started to come down in sheets. All four of us quickly entered the vehicle. Once we had located our Dodge Journey, I deactivated the alarm and unlocked it before getting out. I was prepared to drive by myself until I saw Diego hop out and run to the passenger side of the vehicle. We both climbed inside, a little damp, but no worse for the wear.

"I thought you were going to ride with them," I said nonchalantly.

"I can leave if you want me to," he teased, laughing.

I laughed with him. "No, you can stay," I replied noncommittally.

"Why do you seem so angry?" he questioned.

"I'm not so much angry as I am disappointed." I followed Carl out of the lot.

"Then why are you disappointed?" From the corner of my eye, I noticed Diego was looking at me.

"Because this was supposed to be a girls-only weekend, and it hasn't worked out that way at all. And because I'm afraid Shell's in over her head, *way* over her head. I don't know what she was thinking getting involved with a married man."

"Maybe she wasn't trying to think. Maybe she was just trying to feel something instead; something good. From what I hear, her home life is not the best," he countered.

Diego was probably right, and while I felt for Shell, I didn't think messing around with a married man was the best way to deal with her domestic non-bliss.

"I just don't see this ending well, especially for Shell."

"I don't see the problem."

I couldn't believe he had just said that.

"What part of *they are both married* are you not getting?"

"Well, if it's not bothering them, why is it bothering you?"

"Because Shell's not thinking with a clear head, so I have to."

"For someone who's her friend, you sure are acting like her mother."

I shrugged. "Even though I'm only thirteen years older than her, she sometimes sees me as a mother figure. I guess I ran with it."

"You're not her mother, and she's a grown woman. You're not responsible for her, nor are you responsible for her actions. If there's any fallout, although I'm not saying there will be, it will be on Shell and Carl."

I knew Diego was absolutely right, but I was still having a hard time dealing with it. If I really thought about it, I *was* angry. Angry with Shell for allowing herself to get caught up with a married man; angry with Carl for taking advantage of her vulnerabilities; and angry with myself for not nipping it in the bud before it really began, like I really could, though. Shell was going to carry on with this cockamamie plan no matter what I said.

"Are you angry with me?" Diego asked after a few minutes of silence.

I eyed him for a split second, my main focus on the road ahead. Traffic on the highway had slowed considerably because of the rain.

"No, I'm not mad at you. You were right. I need to take a step back, let them handle it, and let the chips fall where they may. But don't let it go to your head," I quipped.

"Which one?" he asked, a mischievous glint in his eye.

I shook my head and laughed. "Neither."

People were pulling off to the side of the road. One thing I realized living in the South was that many of the people were afraid to drive in inclement weather. Being a Northerner, it didn't bother me one bit. Although I slowed my pace because of the traffic in front of me, I kept on going. I wanted to get to our destination as soon as possible.

"Diego?"

"Yes?"

"Can I ask you a question?" Even though I tried to let it go, I was still concerned about Shell.

"Ask me anything."

I'd have to remember later on that he said that.

"We touched on this a bit last night, but you never gave me a straight answer. What made Carl approach Shell? Bottom line is I don't want her to get hurt."

Diego took his eyes off of the road to look at me.

"I'm not going to get into particulars, but like Shell, Carl has his own domestic issues. But believe me, if I thought he was out of line in any way, or was going to do something to put Shell in harm's way, I'd check him myself."

I felt a bit better after Diego said that, but not by much. I still had a nagging feeling in the pit of my stomach that even after tonight, this would be far from over.

Chapter 15

Diego

Torrential rains tore through Hilton Head. The once beautiful white sandy beaches had been turned to mulch as the rain soaked the place. I stared at the TV over the bar as the meteorologist said the rain wouldn't let up until the next day. It was so dark and gloomy that it looked more like ten at night than five in the afternoon.

We were sitting in HH Prime, the beachside dining establishment inside the Omni. On most days you could enjoy dinner while your sensory and olfactory systems enjoyed the sounds and smells of the ocean. The different shades of chocolate brought out the mocha-colored carpet on the floor. The murmurs of other patrons almost drowned out the sounds of the TV. Glasses clinked together as bartenders filled drink orders, which blended with the sounds of servers setting plates and bowls on tables.

"So, we're stuck here," Gabby stated more than asked.

I watched as she swirled her finger around in her water. Everything she did was like seduction. She tilted her head to the side and narrowed her gaze at the TV. Even though she was doing something akin to scowling, it was sexy. I was trying to sit and figure out exactly what was going on with me. I'd met the woman less than forty-eight hours ago, and I couldn't figure her out. Normally, I'd have a woman dead to rights within the first few hours.

"Looks like it," I answered her.

She sighed and shook her head. In my mind, I imagined her silently cursing her friend Shell for getting her stuck on rainy Hilton Head.

"We're stuck out here with no clothes and no toiletries," she fussed.

"There is a little gift shop around the corner that sells toiletries. There is also a shop right down the street. Maybe later, if the rain lets up even an inch, we can go there and get you something. If not, there *is* a laundry room. You can use my room to shower and relax until your clothes are done."

Gabby turned those sultry doelike eyes my way and smirked a bit. "You just have the answer to everything, don't you?"

I shrugged. "I like to be prepared for anything."

"Duly noted. Thanks for the offer," she said, then turned back to the TV.

I thumbed my nose. I guess what was puzzling me was the fact that she acted as if this morning hadn't happened. It was like we were back to being strangers. She didn't act as if the sex between us had been worth talking about, which was different. Anytime I'd had one-night stands before, all they could talk about was what we'd done. That was one of the reasons I started leaving before they could wake up or jetted no sooner than we were done.

"I take it that means you'd rather not be here," I commented.

"What gave me away? The fact that I told you that on the way here?"

I chuckled at her sarcasm. Carl and Shell had disappeared to the spa once they'd gotten here. Who knew what they had talked about and decided on their way over. All I knew was Carl didn't seem to be letting the fact that he was hurt behind what Dali had done to him show. I knew my friend. Knew for a fact that behind this façade was the hurt that the woman he loved hadn't loved him the way he'd thought.

To be honest, I was a bit tickled at the whole thing. Not because I was happy about his pain, but because it had taken him this long to get what I'd been trying to tell him since the day he'd met Dali.

"What's so funny?" Gabby asked me.

I pulled my vibrating phone from my hip . . . frowned when I saw Ricki calling me again. That was twice in one day. What in hell was wrong with her? I glanced up at Gabby.

I shrugged. "Just thinking about something with Carl."

She quirked a brow. "Since my friend is with Carl, should I know why you're laughing?"

I thought about it for a minute. "I'm not sure."

"What does that mean?" she asked.

I sent Ricki to voice mail, laid my phone on the bar, then took a sip of my Hennessey on ice.

"I'm just surprised he picked her out of all the other women in the club."

Gabby cocked her head to the side, set her glass down slowly, and glowered at me. "And just what in blazes is that supposed to mean? Are you saying something is wrong with Shell?"

I chuckled at her readiness to defend her friend. "When it comes to that ninja, yeah."

"What's wrong with Shell? I *know* you're *not* trying to say she's ugly, because you'd be a cotton-picking liar."

I threw my head back and let out a throaty laugh. "Cotton-picking? Really? What the hell?"

"Yes, I said cotton-picking. I happen not to use vulgarity to express myself if that's okay with you. Now, what about Shell makes it so hard to believe Carl picked her, like he's some almighty prize?"

"She's black."

Gabby jerked her head back like she had been slapped. She gave me that black woman glare that would send most men running for the hills.

"*Excuse* me?" she retorted. "Say that again."

"She's black. Carl doesn't usually go for black women."

Gabby gave me a slow blink, then a blank stare. "But . . . Carl's black. As a matter of fact, he's black in race, ethnicity, *and* color. You mean to tell me a man as black as him doesn't date black women?"

"Carl hasn't seen a black twat since one pushed him out."

"You're kidding, right?"

I turned my lips down and shook my head. "Nope."

"So his wife is not black?"

"Not at all."

She looked to be genuinely offended. You would have thought I'd just told her Carl was a convicted murderer and rapist who just escaped from prison.

"I don't know what to say to that. I just don't."

"Me either. Black men who don't date black women confuse me too. Not to say that I have anything against it. I just don't get going out of your way to date someone who doesn't look like your mother."

She nodded, then asked the bartender for a Mojito with black salt before she commented. "I'll agree with you there. I don't either. Makes me wonder."

"About what?"

"Why Carl picked Shell."

"Misery loves company, and they seem to be having a great time."

She chuckled lightly as she shook her head. Her locs swayed against her back, drawing my attention to her backside on the stool.

"If you take a picture; it'll last longer," she said.

I looked back up at her to see she wasn't even watching me. Her eyes were back on the TV.

"How do you know what I'm looking at? You're not even watching me."

"I know you see it. You can't help it. You're a man of color. It attracts you like honeybees to flowers and nectar."

"Bees to honey, you mean?"

She set her glass down and turned to me. "Bees are attracted to flowers and nectar. They make the honey from the nectar and pollenate other flowers with the pollen they get from another. Therefore, you're attracted to a nice round backside like honeybees are attracted to flowers and nectar. Or would like a moth to a flame be better suited to your understanding?" she asked, then shrugged. "It's in your blood, unless you're like your boy Carl."

I didn't know what to make of all she'd just said. On one hand, I could have taken offense to the way she'd just tried to school me. On the other hand, I could be turned on by the fact that she had a smirk on her face as she visually drank me in. I couldn't be mad at her, though, not when my eyes were feasting on everything that made her a woman. Either way, with Gabby's high cheekbones, she had a naturally smiling mouth. So it was hard to tell whether she was really being snide or not. I could tell her cynical mood was only a defense mechanism, and I was okay with that.

"I'm black, so black women suit me just fine," I assured her.

"You identify as black?"

My brows furrowed. "What else am I supposed to identify as?"

"I mean, just looking at you, I wasn't really sure, and I know how a lot of Latinos shy away from that side of who they are."

"Not me. My pops raised me to be very proud of who I am."

She nodded but didn't say anything else about it. Once the bartender gave her the drink she'd ordered, I told her to put it on my tab, but Gabby stopped me.

"Thank you, but I got it," she told me.

"You sure?"

"Yes."

The bartender didn't know what to do as she looked from me to Gabby. Gabby handed her a twenty and told her to keep the change. I really wanted to go upstairs to my room and take a nap, but had decided to stay seated at the bar to keep Gabby company when it was certain that Shell was going to run off with Carl. I didn't want to leave her hanging.

My mind drifted back to Ricki, and I had to wonder if she was about to be tossed aside like all the other women who'd made the mistake of getting too attached. But then again, it was unlike her to call me more than once in a day so I wanted to make sure she was okay.

I sent her a text: You okay?

I looked up when the lights flickered on and off in the place. Someone squealed. The bartender jumped and looked around. A few people took that as their cue to leave. My palms started to sweat and heart started to race.

"We can go up to the room if you want," I told Gabby. "And don't worry, I'm not trying to have sex with you. Just wouldn't want you to be caught down here when the lights go out."

Well, some of that was the truth. While I wouldn't want her to get caught down here alone, it would be great to have her in my room. The woman was fine, and she was an authentic black woman . . . the locs, the fresh glowing face free of makeup, and an ass that swayed to the tune of African and Cuban drums each time she walked. The turquoise color against her chocolate skin made the air around her electric for me.

I couldn't understand for the life of me what would make Carl not appreciate the beauty in a black woman.

"You want to take a walk?" I asked Gabby.

"To where? It's raining like heck out there."

I inwardly chuckled at her word usage again. "You're natural anyway. Little rain won't hurt. We can walk out to the deck, then find a dry spot in the cabana to chill and watch the way the lightning dances on the ocean."

She finished her drink and left the bartender another tip. I told the bartender to close my tab. Signed the receipt and left a nice tip of my own. Gabby grabbed up her purse. I asked her to put my phone inside of it so it wouldn't get wet. She did. We made our way through the crowd in the lobby, then swung around by the elevators. Looked like the power surge had put it out of business for a minute. There was crowd gathered there as well. While people were rushing inside from the entrance, I pushed the door open for Gabby so we could head out. We passed by the kids club and spa lounging area. Could see the golf course in the distance.

Luckily, the walkway was covered overhead. The wind still pushed some of the pelts of rain our way but not enough to drench us. That didn't happen until we got to the deck. I'd always been a fan of rain. Something about it was tranquilizing for me. A stroll in the rain made it all the better, unless it was freezing cold. And that was what Savannah had decided to dump on us. I held my jacket over her head as we rushed into the cabana. Good thing it was being kept warm by heaters. No one was there besides the cabana boy. We'd been the only ones crazy enough to do so. Another thing about Gabby that drew me to her. She was daring.

Once we made it to one of the plush white seats, the cabana boy got busy pulling down the covers on the side and zipping them to close us in. He asked us if we needed anything.

"No, thank you. I'm fine," Gabby told him with a smile.

"I'm cool," I told him.

"I'll be here if you need me, but just a memo . . . If the elements get too harsh, we'll have to head in," the blond kid told us.

I nodded as I handed Gabby one of the white towels to wipe the water from her face and neck.

"Too harsh?" she repeated. "What do they call this?"

All I did was chuckle. Couldn't do much else when her baby doll blouse was sticking to her chest. A lace bra that matched the color of her shirt could be seen, along with the dark areola and hardened nipples. She caught me looking. I apologized.

She grunted, then inhaled and exhaled hard. "You do know I'm only keeping you company so Shell won't think I'm trying to spoil her fun, right?"

"Really?"

"Yes, really."

"So what about last night?"

She gave a quick shake of her head and an aggravated shrug. "What about it?"

"You had to have sex with me to keep me company?"

"I had sex with you because you were offering it."

"I was offering it?"

"Yeah. You were being a typical male. You know you're attractive. Probably used to getting whatever you want. So, I figured if you were going to give it away, why not take it. It was just one night anyway, right?"

If I hadn't been so taken aback by her assessment, I probably would have laughed.

"So is that why you were so quick to go back on your stance of no one-night stands?"

She stood, unbuttoned her shirt showing perky brown breasts, that turquoise lace bra, and toned abs. She was in tip-top shape, but that feminism that made her a woman was still intact.

She took another towel and wiped herself down as she told me, "No, but I figured if I was going to go there, it may as well have been with someone who looked decent."

"Just decent?"

She stopped wiping away the moisture and tossed the towel in the wicker basket. "Are you fishing for a compliment, Diego?" she asked with an alluring smile.

I stood, pulled my shirt over my head, then my tee shirt. "No, but saying I'm decent isn't the best way to describe a person's looks."

I grabbed up a towel to wipe my face again. Then did the same as she'd just done. I wiped away the water that had soaked my upper body. I looked over at her to find she was watching me. I smirked.

"Take a picture; it'll last longer," I told her, mocking her words to me earlier.

She shook her head. "You take the cake when it comes to arrogance, you know."

"This coming from the woman who told me because I was a man of color I couldn't help but be attracted to her ass. Like honeybees to flowers and nectar you said."

She ignored what I said, then walked up to me and touched the scar on my chest. A burn from a space heater when I was a kid had left me with a nice set of bars over my heart. Her delicate fingers brushed across the scar ever so lightly. She'd taken notice of it last night as well, but I guess we were too caught up for her to say anything then.

"First, you tell me I'm not attractive, and then you touch me without asking," I said while gazing down at her.

She moved her hand. "You're spoiled, aren't you?"

"What's that got to do with anything?"

"A lot."

I reached out to move her closer to me, but she backed away. Started to button her shirt as she did, then took a seat on the cushioned bench. I decided to leave my shirt off for the time being. I walked to sit next to her. We kept the conversation light. Talked about the beauty of a storm. Watched as lightning skittered across the ocean. She told me how, even though she didn't condone Shell's action, that she was glad her friend was having fun.

We talked briefly about the games men and women played in relationships. I asked her why she wasn't afraid her ex might go all *Southern Fried Homicide* on her since she was such a big fan of the show.

She laughed. "He's stupid, but he isn't crazy. I will go above and beyond to defend myself. Believe that."

I chuckled as I stretched, then yawned. "You want to go back in?" I asked her.

"No, but looks like you do."

"I am a little tired. Some little lady kept me up all night."

"Really now? Is that good or bad?"

I gave her a once-over. Cursed myself for letting her take me out of my element. Damned my dick to hell for coming to life at the thought of feeling the insides of her womanhood again.

"Are you fishing for compliments, Gabrielle?"

Her slinky smile was back. She placed her fingers back on the scar over my heart. She was smiling, but there was a serious gaze in her eyes.

"There are bars over your heart. Maybe this was a foreshadow of the future."

I didn't understand. I told her as much.

"You're forty. No kids. No woman. No marriage. You've gone and put bars over your heart, and nobody has the key to unlock them."

I frowned a bit, then moved her hand. "Thank you, Dr. Psycho-Analyzer. I appreciate your diagnosis. However, I'll have to disagree."

"Denial isn't just a river in Egypt, my good man," she replied, tapping the scar on my chest.

I didn't respond. Didn't get a chance to. The cabana boy put us off the island. We headed back into the hotel. Not wanting to wait in line for the elevator, Gabby suggested we take the stairs back up to my suite. I didn't have a problem with that . . . until we got in the stairwell and the lights went out. I stopped. Closed my eyes, then leaned against the wall.

"Diego, you okay?" Gabby asked me.

I didn't even front or try to lie. I wasn't okay. I had been afraid of the dark since I'd tripped over my pop's toolbox when I five. I fell chest first over that space heater and listened to the skin sizzle off my chest. As much as a man I prided myself to be, turning the lights out like this took me back to that moment. I mean, I didn't have a problem with regular darkness, you know, the kind of dark where you could still see the things around you, but pitch-black darkness, the kind where you couldn't even see your hand in front of your face, was something else altogether. I opened my eyes and couldn't see my own fingers in front of me. I could hear Gabby searching around in her purse. She pulled out my cell because I could see the missed texts from Ricki when the screen lit up. She held it up to my face.

"You okay?" Her eyes held concerned.

I shook my head and slowly plopped down on the steps with my head against the wall. "Don't like the dark," I told her. "Fucking heater . . . was trying to get to my parents . . . tripped in the dark. Fell on that fucking space heater. I don't fuck with the dark like this."

I probably sounded like the biggest damned punk God had ever created. Not even Carl knew about my fear of the dark. I kept it that way. My hands started to shake. Knees started to feel like rubber. As soon as I thought I was about to let anxiety turn me into an even bigger pussy, Gabby's lips found mine. My hands fisted as a different kind of anxiety came over me.

She moaned while she kissed me. Made me feel like I'd tiptoed out of hell right into the clouds of heaven. She kissed me like that for maybe a good ten minutes. I could feel and hear her moving around anxiously. Once my hands grabbed bare hips, I knew she had been removing her tights. Shit. Gabby was an enigma. I hadn't expected this part at all. Hands touching, roaming around my chest, she straddled my lap.

She went for my belt buckle, and I stopped her. "What if somebody comes through here?"

She giggled a bit. "Diego, you don't come across as someone who's afraid of a little public sex. With all that 'decent' game you were spitting last night, I didn't take you for a cautious kind of man, at least not in this aspect. Look, the lights are out, elevators are down. Nobody is thinking of coming up or down these stairs."

She was right, and I'd only been apprehensive because I didn't want her to get caught. Hell, for that matter, my black ass didn't want to be caught either. No matter how adventurous we were didn't mean other people would like to see it. But I forgot all about that once she released me from my slacks and boxer briefs. She pulled out a condom. Slid off me to get down on her knees. I couldn't see her face, but I could feel when she used her mouth to slide the condom into place. The heat from her mouth was blinding.

I damn near lost my mind when she rubbed the head of my dick up and down her slit. I used my head to rap against her clit as she hissed and moaned. My hands found her shirt. Quickly, I ripped the buttons away, then popped her breasts from her lace bra. My mouth latched on to her nipple greedily. I suckled like I was famished, then hungrily licked around each areola and paid each nipple equal attention.

I brought her face close to mine and kissed her lips. Then I softly licked on her neck and suckled right where I could tell her sensitive spot was. Anytime my tongue touched that spot, her hand stroking got more intense, her breathing got more erratic. She lifted her hips and guided me home just as my lips found her earlobe.

Damn.

She brought her lips to my neck and gave me soft, feathery bites that made my high that much more potent. She rocked her hips against mine in a steady beat. Rode me like she knew we had to get to our destination fast. We didn't have that much time. I was sure the generators for such an establishment would kick in soon enough. I held her hips and took control. Bounced her up and down to match my thrusts. She handled it. Took it all. Gave little whimpers that told of her enjoyment. I gritted my teeth, then bit down on my bottom lip when I felt the tension in my balls accelerate.

"I'm coming. Oh . . . man . . . I'm coming so hard," she crooned next to my ear.

I was too. She lay her head on my shoulder and moved her ass and hips in a dirty whine that would make men in the islands proud. I shot off like a rocket.

The lights came back on just as we were fixing our clothes. She put her boyshorts in her purse, grabbed a wipe, and used it to remove the used condom from my semi-hardened phallus. She was careful as she balled it in her hand. Once I was all put together, she handed it to me.

"I'm not carrying your kids, mister," she quipped, then winked.

I laughed as we headed out of the stairwell, leaving the scent of our stolen quickie behind.

Chapter 16

Carl

I had every intention of getting Shell alone again. I was pretty sure Diego would have no objections to hitting the sheets with Gabby either. She was pissed off because she and Shell were stuck here due to the storm, but knowing Diego, I was more than confident that he could sweet-talk her out of her panties, just like he did last night. The brother could sweet-talk the panties off of a nun.

I figured since we were on lockdown for the duration, we might as well enjoy it. As soon as we got to the hotel, Shell and I excused ourselves. I had big plans for her.

"Where are we going, Carl?" she questioned.

"You'll see," I said, taking her by the hand.

We reached the front desk and were greeted by an overly friendly desk clerk. "Good afternoon and how may I help you?"

His overexuberant customer service smile was a bit over the top. He reminded me of Richie Cunningham from *Happy Days*.

"Yes . . . Johnnie," I paused, looking at his name tag. "I'm Carl Robinson, and I'm staying in suite 501," I said, showing him my room key. "My wife Mischelle just arrived, and I need to get her checked in."

The look of shock on Shell's face told me that I probably should have warned her before saying she was my wife, but it was too late for that. I was in the moment, and she needed to keep up.

"Sure thing, Mr. Robinson. I'll just issue you another room key. Does Mrs. Robinson have any bags she would like the valet to take upstairs?"

"No, I'm here on business, and I had the wife join me unexpectedly. I'm taking her to the boutique to go shopping."

"Wise choice, sir. Also, I see you upgraded to the Cabana Sea Breeze Package. Your bottle of wine will be delivered shortly, and you both will have breakfast in the Palmetto Café tomorrow morning. Would you like me to schedule a massage now?"

"Yes, thank you. What's the availability?"

Johnnie tapped away on his keyboard, looking at the screen.

"Well, Mr. Robinson, the earliest we can get you in is one hour from now. Is that acceptable?"

"That would be fine."

I figured Shell would need that amount of time to go shopping.

"Would that be a massage for just your wife or a couple's massage?"

"Couple's massage."

"And would you like fifty or eighty minutes?"

I thought about it. The more time I had alone with Shell the better. "Fifty is good."

"And, sir, is the number we have on file your home or cell phone number?"

"Cell."

"Okay, then, we have you and Mrs. Robinson scheduled for one hour from now for a fifty-minute couple's massage. The spa will call you fifteen minutes beforehand to remind you. Anything else for you, Mr. Robinson?"

"No, that's it. Thanks."

"And thank you for staying at the Omni. If there's anything else you need, please feel free to let us know," Johnnie said, still over the top.

As we stepped away from the front desk, Shell stopped me.

"Carl, why did you say I was your wife?"

"Would you prefer I said you were my mistress? Or maybe the woman I met and slept with less than twenty-four hours ago?" I quipped.

"Not funny. I was just asking a question. You don't have to be an ass about it," she said, pouting.

I replied, "I've been called worse. Now, come on."

She stood firm. "No. Not until you tell me why you're doing all this."

Sighing, I asked her, "Do you remember what I said to you when we were in the parking lot last night?"

She paused, as if searching her memories. "Carl, you said a lot of things last night. Please just tell me."

I could tell she wasn't in the mood for games, so I begrudgingly relented. "I told you we could pretend that I'm your husband and you're my wife, and all I wanted to do was make you happy. And that's what I intend to do. Now, follow me."

I took her by the hand, first leading her to the Palmetto Market to buy some toiletries. We then headed to Omni Shores, the hotel's exclusive boutique.

Shell stopped at the entrance as if a barrier was in front of her. "What are you waiting for?" I questioned.

"I can't afford any of this," she protested.

"You can't, but I can," I countered.

A saleswoman approached us. "Hi. Welcome to Omni Shores. My name is Tracey. Can I help you find something?"

"Yes, Tracey, my wife needs a few things. Can you help her out?" I reached in my wallet, pulling out my American Express Centurion Card, handing it to her.

She looked at it, saying, "Yes, Mr. Robinson. Whatever she needs." She smiled, then said to Shell, "Mrs. Robinson, please come with me. Anything in particular . . ." her voice trailed off as she led Shell through the store.

I took a seat in the waiting area, checking my messages. Dali continued to call and text. Just like before, she got no response. I also received a text message from my sister, Anastasia, or Ana, for short. She was the second-oldest sibling, being ten years my junior at thirty years old. She was about to graduate from Columbia University with a Ph.D. in pharmacology. I was very proud of her. Her text was simply a heart; her way of telling me she loved me. I responded in kind.

Despite our age difference, Ana and I were pretty close. So much so that when one of her ex-boyfriends attempted to put his hands on her, I was the first person she called. Needless to say, after the ass whooping I gave him, he never bothered her again.

I had four other siblings. Twenty-seven year old Porshia was a graduate student at the Fashion Institute of Technology studying Global Fashion Management. Malina, twenty-five, worked as a nurse in the neonatal intensive care unit at NYU Langone Medical Center. My nineteen-year-old brother Darian was still trying to find himself, but his time was running out. I told him he had one year after high school to make a decision about what he wanted to do with his life. After that, he either had to go to school or find a job, because he would not be living off of my mother, which essentially meant living off of me. The baby of the family, Nathaniel, was fifteen. He was a freshman in a very exclusive prep school.

I gave all my siblings the same deal; do well in school with nothing less than a B+ average and I would fully subsidize them. All their needs were covered by me, including clothing, tuition, books, electronics, and an allowance to cover day-to-day expenses. I even bought the older ones co-ops close to school in order to decrease travel time.

I made them all sign contracts agreeing to my terms. I had full access to their online grades. That way, I could keep track of them. If they fell short, they knew the consequences. Allowances would be decreased and certain privileges would be revoked until grades came back up. And if they didn't come back up, they would eventually be cut off. Luckily, I never had to go that far.

Some may have thought my methods were harsh, but I saw it as making sure my sisters and brothers lived up to their fullest potential. I wanted them to make the most of the opportunities presented to them, like I did.

Unfortunately, I couldn't do the same for my mother. Raped by her mother's husband from the time she was ten, she never really had a chance to see what life had to offer. Her stepfather got her pregnant when she was only thirteen, then made her get an abortion. After that, she stayed in one dysfunctional relationship after another, including the one she had with my sperm donor, a married man who played on her daddy issues and knocked her up when she was fifteen.

Even her relationship with her own mother was dysfunctional. Mom claims that woman didn't know about the abuse. I call bullshit. There was no way she couldn't have known what was going on, living in a small, two-bedroom shack in Mississippi. That's why, to this day, if that bitch was on fire, I wouldn't spit on her to help her out. And that son-of-a-bitch sperm donor of mine . . . let's just say I better not ever see him on the street.

Because of everything that she went through, I didn't press Mom too hard. Even though I had to take responsibility for the household, becoming the man of house way too early, I understood why she was the way she was. I got used to managing her money in order to make sure all the bills were paid, there was food on the table, and everyone had clothes on their backs. I organized the house so everyone got up on time for school every morning, did their chores, and had their homework done before bedtime, all the while still going to school myself. As they say, I pulled myself up by my bootstraps, so my brothers and sisters had no excuse for not doing the same.

To hear Diego tell it, that was why I never dated black women; because they reminded me too much of my mother and my fucked-up childhood. He had been saying that for years. Personally, I think he's full of shit, but he is entitled to his opinion.

I was pulled out of my thoughts by the vibration of my phone. It was Dali . . . again. Dammit. I answered in the hopes that she was agreeing to the terms of the divorce. No such luck.

"Yeah," I answered dryly.

"Hello, Carl. I was just checking to see if you had a chance to think about what I had said earlier."

I took a deep breath, not wanting to show my natural ass in the boutique. "There's nothing to think about. I want a divorce, plain and simple."

"But, Carl, why would you want to throw away seventeen years of marriage?"

Was this bitch *really* asking me that? To hell with showing my ass. I stepped outside.

"Why would *I* throw away seventeen years? *You* did that shit, Dali, not me. *You're* the one who destroyed our marriage. Do us both a favor and stop calling me with this bullshit before I say something I definitely will not regret." I gave her the dial tone. Then I proceeded to block her calls and text messages.

As I walked back into the boutique, Shell was coming toward the front of the store. She observed the look of irritation on my face. "What's wrong?"

"Nothing. What's up?"

She opened her mouth to say something, then stopped. I could tell she wanted to press me further, but thought better of it, instead, continuing with her reason for seeking me out.

"Uh, Carl, yeah, about these prices, I can get a full wardrobe at Walmart for the price of *one* of these items."

"Your point being?" I queried, once again taking a seat.

"These things are really expensive."

"Again, so what's your point?" I folded my hands, resting my chin on them.

"Carl—"

I had had my fill of Walmart growing up. At one point, things had gotten so bad that, aside from food, we had to buy mostly everything else on layaway. Which was why I had an aversion to shopping there now.

"Look, Shell," I said, cutting her off, "I told you I was going to treat you like you're my wife. Well, this is how I treat my wife. You can shop at Walmart on your own time, but right now, you're on mine, so run along," I said, shooing her away, a smile on my face.

"Fine," she muttered, walking away.

A few minutes later she returned. She tried on one dress, modeled it for me, asking my opinion.

"Nah, looks like a muumuu."

She put her hands on her full hips, glowering at me. Then she gave me the finger.

"Later," I said, laughing.

When she came back, she had on a sea-foam-green sundress. It was very flattering, showing off her cleavage, thick hips, and round ass. "Yeah, I like that," I said appraisingly.

"Figures," she teased. "It shows off my boobs."

"Yes, it does. And the view from here is outstanding."

She rolled her eyes, sticking her tongue out at me before walking back to the fitting room.

"I'm going to hold you to that," I yelled.

By the time Shell was done, she had picked out two bras with matching boyshorts, a red and white tank top, a pair of red capris, the sundress, a pair of silver thong sandals, and a silver jewelry set consisting of a matching bracelet, necklace, and earrings. Just as we walked up to the register, my phone rang. It was the spa reminding us that our appointment was in fifteen minutes.

"Will there be anything else for you, Mr. and Mrs. Robinson?"

I looked at Shell, making sure she was satisfied with what she had picked out.

"I'm good," she stated.

"Thank you, Tracey, that will be all," I said.

Once she rang up the purchases, Shell and I took her bags to the room before walking over to Hilton Head's Luxury Spa Resort. Upon our arrival, we were greeted by two staff members, one male, one female. The female spoke up. "Good afternoon. Mr. and Mrs. Robinson?"

"Yes," I replied.

"Welcome to Hilton Head's Luxury Spa Resort. My name is Miranda, and this is Rob. We'll be giving you your massages today. If you will follow us, we will take you to your room."

As we passed through the main sitting area, I noticed the furniture color scheme of blues, browns, and tans. It blended well with the camel-colored carpet. The chairs were all loungers, some that were extra long, and some with removable ottomans. They all had several throw pillows and a blanket on them.

Miranda led us into a room that contained two massage tables with two work tables set up next to them. The work tables contained what I assumed were massage oils. "You can change in here. Rob and I will be back in a few minutes," she said, closing the door behind her.

Shell looked at me, a smile on her face.

"What?" I asked.

"I'm just having a good time is all," she said, attempting to cover up as she changed her clothes.

"I don't know why you're doing that now," I chided. "I've already seen your goods," I said playfully, taking off my clothes.

I could have sworn I made her blush. We both put our clothes neatly on the two chairs at opposite ends of the small room. Just as we climbed onto the massage tables and covered ourselves with the sheets provided, we heard a knock on the door.

"Come in," Shell said.

Miranda and Rob reentered the room, closing the door behind them. "Mr. and Mrs. Robinson, you're in for a real treat. Our couple's massage is a classic therapeutic, Swedish-style massage that uses light to moderate touch performed in synchronized unison. When we're done, you'll be left feeling relaxed, refreshed, and rejuvenated. Now, for your music, would you prefer New Age, classical, or smooth jazz?"

"Smooth jazz, thank you," I replied.

"Okay, well, let's get started."

I wasn't really one for getting a massage, but after the past few months I had, I needed something to relax. As Miranda worked her magic, I started to feel my stress fade away, all the bullshit in my life taking a backseat for the moment. Before closing my eyes, I looked over at Shell. She already had her eyes closed. She looked very peaceful.

Before I knew it, I heard a bell go off indicating the end of our session.

"Mr. and Mrs. Robinson, our time is up. On behalf of Rob and myself, we would like to thank you for staying at the Omni," Miranda said. "We don't need the room for another thirty minutes, so please feel free to take your time getting dressed. Enjoy the rest of your stay."

With that, she and Rob exited, leaving Shell and me alone.

I sat up, then climbed down from the massage table, walked to the chair containing my clothes, and pulled out my wallet, placing a twenty-dollar bill in the envelopes sitting on each work table. Shell finally rose, looking very relaxed. She took a long stretch, causing the sheet she was wrapped in to fall lower on her breasts. I walked over to her.

"Feeling good?" I asked.

"Very good," she replied, a look of contentment on her face.

"I can make you feel even better. Let me give you a happy ending," I said, pulling the sheet down further, fully exposing her abundant breasts. I placed my hands over each nipple, massaging them.

"Carl, we can't. They'll be back soon," she said, her body betraying her, as she closed her eyes, a soft moan escaping her lips.

"We have thirty minutes. That's plenty of time," I said.

One hand still fondled her breasts, while the other reached under the sheet. Using my knee, I parted her thighs, then ran a finger up and down her damp slit. When I inserted it between her folds, it caused her to hiss. My thumb ran across her clit. Her head went back as she bit her bottom lip. I continued to caress her breasts, all the while finger fucking her and teasing her clit. I could tell by the way her pussy was starting to pulse that she was going to come soon.

I wanted to put my dick inside her so badly my balls ached. We didn't have enough time for that now, but we would later.

I leaned in close, whispering in her ear, "Has your husband ever made you feel this?"

"What?" She opened her eyes, a confused look on her face.

I looked her squarely in the eyes. "You heard me. Has your husband ever made you feel like this?"

"Yes . . . well, no," she panted.

I inserted another finger and quickened my strokes.

"That's what I thought. When you get back home and you're in your bed at night, I want you to remember who made you feel like this, remember who made your pussy wet like this," I baited. I felt her walls contract as she buried her face in my chest, stifling her screams of passion. "And remember who made you come like this."

I only stopped once her body stopped shaking. When she was done, I removed my fingers from her sopping wet pussy, lifting her chin up with my other hand. I kissed her slowly.

"Now, get dressed," I told her, just as everything went dark.

Chapter 17

Mischelle

A blackout? I couldn't believe it. I rushed to put my clothes back on. One of the masseuses had come back in to inform us of the power outage in the hotel. My lady parts were soaking wet because Carl had decided to play hide-and-seek with his fingers inside of me.

"Don't panic," Carl said to me. "A place like this should have backup generators or something."

"I'm not panicking. I just need to be sure Gabby's okay."

"Why wouldn't she be? She's with Diego."

"What's that mean? I still need to be sure she's okay."

I could hear Carl's belt buckle clinking as he pulled his pants on. Since the massage room had little candles lit about, we weren't in total blackness. Once dressed, he took my hand and led me from the room. I liked that about Carl. He was always in control. Never seemed flustered. Even though he made it known his marriage was on the rocks, he didn't seem fazed.

"Why not just use your cell?"

"It's dead."

"Diego and I are on the same floor. When we get to the room, we can call his room to see if she's there. Cool?" he asked me as we made our way to the elevators.

It took us a minute to get on as the elevator line was long and the electricity was out so the line wasn't moving.

By the time the lights had come back up, the staff of the Omni was walking around apologizing for the inconvenience, assuring everyone that they had everything covered. We hopped on the elevator with about seven other people. It was a tight squeeze. Carl stood against the back wall and pulled me against him. I felt a little flushed. I could feel his manhood pressed against my back. One arm was wrapped around my waist like I belonged to him.

Shell, what in hell are you doing? I asked myself.

Having fun?

Playing with fire?

What?

I had no answers for the questions floating around in my head. All I knew in that moment was that Carl's protective hold felt good to me. It made me feel safe. It had been awhile since Malik had held me that way. The elevator dinged for the fifth floor. Carl and I waited for everyone else to get off before we did. We walked hand in hand down the hall.

"How old are you?" I asked him out of the blue.

He looked down at me. "Forty. Why?"

Both my brows rose. "You're forty?"

I looked him up and down. Damn, forty was looking like that these days? I thought. I guess the old adage good black don't crack was real.

"Yes, I am. Why?"

"No reason."

"You got a problem with me now that you know I'm close to fifty?"

"Nope. I like my men with a little wisdom on them."

He glanced at me. "Oh yeah?"

I nodded. "Gabby always picks on me about it. She asked how I ended up married to Malik."

"I surmise Malik is younger than you?"

Shaking my head, I answered, "No. We're the same age. He's just a few months older."

"So being with an older man has never been an issue for you?"

"Not at all. Something about the age difference that makes the time we spend together more intense."

Carl quirked a brow at me, then smiled.

I giggled a bit and shook my head as he pulled out the electronic key card and slid it into the sleek door slot. The light flashed green, and he pushed the door open to let me walk in first. We had been to the room earlier, but I didn't have a chance to fully take in the room's atmosphere since we were in and out. The room was cool and looked as if it was bigger than my two-bedroom townhome back home. The brown and cream carpet brought out the mocha-colored walls. A burnt-orange chaise with an ottoman sat in front of the glass sliding doors next to a round chocolate wood grain dining table. A square coffee table of the same color sat in front of a burnt-orange sofa. Cream-colored curtains were pulled to the side, showcasing the downpour of rain outside.

The door to the bedroom was open, and I could see the king-size bed had been made. White sheets that looked to be of the highest quality could be seen pulled down and neatly folded over the down comforter. The bed made me want to dive in and sleep away my adulterous ways.

Carl's laptop and electronic tablet sat on the desk by the big flat-screen TV. A pen and a notepad right next to that. I was impressed with the room. The studio-style suite made me wonder what it would be like to live in luxury all the time. I wondered if the day would come when I would ever know what it would feel like not to worry about money.

"You can put your stuff in the closet if you like," Carl said to me.

I nodded and asked, "Hey, will you call Diego to see if Gabby is with him?"

I dropped my bags on the couch and rifled through them, still shocked at the prices on some of the stuff Carl splurged on. Shit, the capris were a hundred and five bucks. For that price, I could get me, Leianni, and Hassan a few outfits. The man was fooling. Spending that much money on clothing seemed asinine to me. The dress he liked so much cost a whopping $200. I had a good mind to take that sucker back.

"Yeah, they did take too long to get the backup generators on. Actually, they should have kicked in immediately," I heard Carl say.

I hopped up and walked into the bedroom. "Gabby with him?" I asked, assuming he was talking to his friend Diego.

He nodded, then told Diego, "Put Gabby on. Shell wants to make sure she's okay."

I eagerly took the phone just as Gabby answered, "Hello."

"You okay?" I wanted to know.

"I'm fine. Meet me in the hall for a second."

"Okay."

I handed the phone back to Carl. Told him I'd be back.

"Where are you going?"

"Just out in the hall to talk to Gabby."

I rushed out and saw Gabby coming from the opposite end of the hall. I couldn't tell what mood she was in just by looking at her. She had her arms folded as it was a bit chilly and had on an oversized tee shirt that I was sure didn't belong to her. Her face was glowing. Although there was no smile on her face, her eyes were shining.

"You okay?" she asked me as she approached.

"I'm good. You get stuck in the restaurant when the lights went out?"

She shook her head. "Was taking the stairs because the lines were too long at the elevator."

I smiled. "You and Diego clicking?"

She shrugged nonchalantly. "Just keeping him company until you come to your senses with Carl."

I chuckled lightly. "You act as if I'm about run off with the man."

"No, *you* act as if you are."

"Just enjoying the moment."

"I can see that."

I chose not to comment on her sarcastic tone and noticed her hair was wet. I asked her about it. She told me she'd gone out in the rain and sat in the cabana with Diego until the rain and wind got to be too much. We stood there laughing and talking a bit. I was doing it to stave off some of the sexual energy Carl had riled up in me.

"So, Diego and I were sitting at the bar talking, and he tells me something interesting about your weekend lover," she said.

Just like my interest piqued, so did the nervousness that had crept up on me.

"Oh God, what is it? He isn't gay, is he?"

Gabby laughed as she shook her head. "No, but, according to Diego, you'd be one on the short list of black women he's ever shown interest in."

My brows furrowed. "Say what?"

"Diego told me that Carl is one of those black men who seem to find his thrill in dating non-black women."

"So that would mean his wife isn't black."

"We can safely assume that."

I shook my head and shifted my weight from one foot to the other. I didn't know how to feel about that tidbit of info. People often called me pro-black because I loved being black. Nothing was more powerful to me than being black and proud. I didn't have anything against interracial dating. I believed love could transcend color. But I did have a problem with the stigmas that came with black men dating "other."

Gabby and I talked a bit more. She wanted to know if I'd planned to stay the night with Carl even if the rain decided to let up.

"Was thinking about it," I told her.

She quirked a brow, then frowned. "How did this go from being a girls' weekend out to you carrying on a weekend affair with a married man?"

"If he'd been single would you be okay with it?"

"No, because we came to get away from men."

I shrugged with a smile. "So, either way, you'd have a problem with it. It's a lose-lose situation."

"Yeah, for me. You're leaving me with no other choice but to share a room with Diego."

"I'm still trying to figure how that is a bad thing, especially since you've already popped the pussy for him."

"Ugh. Goodness, Shell. You don't have to be so crass."

"I'm just saying. Quit fronting like you're not enjoying yourself."

"I didn't say I wasn't. I'm saying I wanted to spend time, chill, kick back, and relax with my girl, but she's too busy popping *her* coochie for Carl."

We both looked at each other and cracked up. I loved Gabby and would always take her advice to heart. I knew what I was doing was wrong, but I didn't care to be right at the moment. I liked the feeling of being pampered and being catered to. Loved the way Carl moved against me when he was inside of me. I had a craving for his sensual foreplay again. Carl was giving me an erotic escapade that I was sure I'd never experience again in my life. And better yet, I loved the distraction he created. Besides, after tonight, I'd never see him again.

"I know I'm wrong," I told Gabby.

She held her hands up. "I'm not here to judge. I'm here to be the voice of reason."

"I know, and I love you for it, but I like pretending to be the wife of a man who pays $200 for one dress."

She rolled her eyes. "So, it's okay for Carl to pay for things you can't afford, but when I offer—"

"Don't even go there. You know why I declined your offer."

She mumbled, "Whatever."

"Anyway. I need to go shower because Carl decided to be nasty in the spa room." I cast a knowing glance at her. "Care to explain why you're wearing Diego's shirt?"

She looked down like she just realized she was wearing the tee shirt that was swallowing her whole.

"Oh," she said flipping her hand off. "My shirt got wet when we went to the cabana. He offered one of his."

I wasn't so sure I believed her. "The Omni Boutique is downstairs. It's a bit expensive, but you can grab another shirt there."

She nodded. "Okay. You go shower, and I'll check the store out."

"Let me know if you want to leave in all seriousness. I won't force you to stay just because I want to be a whore."

Gabby laughed. "Go on, Shell. I need to get to this boutique to see what they have."

"Okay," I said laughing with her.

I walked back in the room to hear the shower already going. I saw a phone charger in the wall and hoped that it would fit mine. Luck was on my side. I hooked my phone up and waited for it to power on.

I looked up just as Carl was walking around the corner, and my breath caught in my throat. He was still wet. A white bath towel was wrapped around his waist as water trickled down his sculpted chest and abs. That white sat out in stark contrast to the chocolate skin he'd been blessed with. His locs rocked and swayed around his shoulders as he looked at me. He didn't have his glasses on, so I got to see those liquid black eyes with no filter.

"You talk to your girl?" he asked me.

I nodded because I couldn't speak. Carl's dark skin was hypnotizing. His eyes pulled me in further into his web of lust. At that point, I didn't give a damn who he was married to or why he'd married her.

"Everything okay with her?"

I answered, "Yes, she's fine." *And so are you,* I quipped mentally.

"Cool. You can shower if you want. I'm hungry so I'm going to order up room service. What do you have in mind to eat?" he asked as he walked over to the table to pick up the room service menu from the restaurant downstairs.

"Steak," I said as I eyed him hungrily.

He looked over at me and smirked, like he picked up on the silent innuendo I'd thrown out.

"Later," was how he answered.

"In that case, I'll have whatever you're having."

He nodded. I got up to shower. As I adjusted the water to the hottest I could stand it, I thought about what would happen after the weekend was over. Carl would go back to his life in New York, and I'd go back to being an unhappily married woman whose husband had cheated and walked out on her. I didn't ask for much. All I wanted was for Malik to be a bit more supportive and attentive. I wanted him to see how I took pride in being his wife. Wanted him to see all the work I put into keeping a home for him and our children. I needed him to acknowledge the fact I was going to school and writing so our kids could have a better upbringing than we had growing up. It was not because I didn't want to spend time with him or be his wife.

I sighed and let the water wash over me as I pulled my braids up into a bun. I took the sponge and washed over my skin. Then I picked up a white washcloth to clean my woman parts. I was all into humming a made-up tune when Carl walked into the bathroom. I watched him snatch the towel from his waist. I couldn't help it. My eyes latched on to what made him a man anatomically.

I got an aching between my thighs that only he could cure. He had one of those dicks that looked like it had been molded by the hands of God himself. I counted four veins that sat out in regal attention. I wanted to run my tongue from the base of his shaft to the mushroom crown of its head. I licked my lips like I could already taste him there. Wasn't sure how I felt about wanting to suck another man off who wasn't my husband.

But I for damn sure was thinking hard about it.

My heart started to race as he slid the shower door back and stepped inside.

"You order the food?" I asked as if the temperature in the room hadn't shot up a notch.

"I did," he answered, then closed the gap between us in the shower.

The sound of the water created an ambiance of being near a waterfall. His big hands held my waist as he gazed down at me, the heady look in his eyes forcing me to look away to get my bearings.

"What did you get?"

"Let it surprise you. Besides, I don't want to hear you complain about what you can't afford and what's too expensive."

I chuckled lightly, placed my arms around his neck. "I'm a country girl who's not used to such frivolous spending."

He smiled . . . more like gave a smirk before dipping his head to take my mouth. Pulling me closer, he let his hands travel over the dip in my back and land on my backside. I could feel him hardening against my stomach. I moaned out loud. Couldn't help it. Carl's tongue was working magic in my mouth. The scent of Dove permeated the space. It tickled my senses as Carl's natural scent intoxicated me.

He pulled back from the kiss, lowered his head, and took one of my breasts into his mouth. My head dropped back while my hands fisted his locs. I loved when a man remembered I had *two* breasts and paid them both the same kind of attention.

When he moved down further, kneeled down in front of me while placing a trail of kisses from the valley between my breasts down my navel, my legs started to shake. He threw my right leg over his shoulder and sucked my clit into his mouth.

I hissed. Gripped his locs tighter. My mouth was open, eyes shut tight as I called on God.

"Shit, Carl . . ."

I glanced down at him to see he was all in. His face smothered in my pussy as his tongue vibrated against the only part of my body made strictly for pleasure. While I was trying to recuperate from the intense feeling of an orgasm on the horizon, he inserted two fingers inside of me. I came instantly, almost slipping in the process because of the quake in my womb.

"Oh my God! Carl, stop. I'm going to f-fall . . . Ahhhhh . . ."

If Malik had walked in right then with a gun aimed at me I wouldn't have been able to stop. I was too far gone. So far gone, in fact, that when Carl stood and lifted me around his waist, I didn't think about the fact he didn't have a condom on. Not until I felt how intense . . . Oh God . . . there he was . . . inside of me . . . raw. I bit down on my bottom lip and growled as I hid my face in his shoulder. I had to stop. We had to stop. He knew it too.

"Shit," I heard him mumble.

Playing with fire was what we were doing. The feel of him inside of me uninhibited made me feel savage. Made me feel as if I was in a mating ritual, one where Carl belonged to me and only me.

"We have to stop . . . condom," I murmured through bated breaths.

"I know," he said.

We were doing wrong. So wrong. Trying to have what couldn't be. I pulled my head up and looked down at him. He'd weakened me. Gotten me to the point that I didn't care about the consequences of my actions. I had to pull back. Needed to be responsible.

"Get a condom, please," I asked of him.

I inhaled hard when he made his dick jump inside of me. Since neither of us were moving, I could feel every pulsating sensation he made inside of me. But he knew we couldn't do this. We couldn't travel a road of *what if* and let the chips fall where they may. He took me from his waist and grabbed my hand as we exited the shower.

"Lie down," he told me.

My body still wet from the shower, I crawled onto the bed. I watched in eager anticipation as he ripped open a condom and expertly rolled it on. My thighs were already open. I was so willing, so ready to let him have me. When he crawled between my thighs . . . caged me between his arms . . . slipped inside of me so agonizingly slow, I knew it was going to be hard to say good-bye when the weekend was over.

Chapter 18

Gabrielle

We were stuck in Hilton Head for the duration. The storm showed no sign of letting up, and even if it did and we had a chance of getting back to Tybee Island, Shell was so caught up playing house with Carl I didn't think I'd be able to separate them with a blowtorch, C4, or dynamite. After our meeting in the hallway, it was evident that she was completely enamored with him. I'd let her live her fantasy of being Mrs. Mischelle Robinson for the duration, because all too soon, we'd be returning to reality.

When I left to talk to Shell, Diego was taking a shower. I got back, and he was already dressed, wearing a white tank top, a pair of white, black, and red basketball shorts; and a pair of white and black Nike Air Max 2015 running shoes. He looked just as good in casual attire as he did in business wear.

"Mind if I take a shower now?"

"It's all yours. I imagine Carl and Shell won't be coming up for air anytime soon," he presumed.

I shook my head. "So it seems. They're in fairy tale lockdown, pretending they're married to each other. Go figure," I shrugged.

"I'm not even going to attempt to try to figure that one out," he said, laughing.

"Agreed. Trying to understand this whole situation is making my brain hurt."

"So don't think about it. You two will be heading back to Tybee Island tomorrow, so whatever is going on between those two will be over. That'll be the end of it," he deduced, grabbing his wallet and keycard off the desk.

"I hope you're right, because I can't take much more of their scandalous lovefest," I said. "Are you going downstairs?" I questioned.

"Yes. I'm going down to the shop. Write down what you want me to pick up," he said, handing me the pad and pen that were sitting on his nightstand.

I took it from him, leaned on the desk, and wrote down all the toiletries I needed.

"I really hate asking you this, but can you do me a huge favor?"

"What is it?" he inquired.

"Shell said there's a boutique downstairs. It's called the Omni Boutique. Would you mind seeing what they have since I don't have a change of clothes?"

"Sure, no problem," he replied. "You actually trust my judgment?"

I shrugged. "Looking at the way you dress yourself, I think you'll pick something nice."

"So you like the way I dress, do you?" he asked, that perfect smile on his face.

"Still fishing for compliments, I see," I teased, pulling Diego's oversized shirt over my head, handing it to him. "I'm going to take my shower."

He licked his lips, looking me up and down. I noticed the already-impressive bulge in his shorts had gotten even larger. "On second thought, I could always go downstairs later. Want some company?"

My body wanted to say yes over and over again, but my common sense was telling me, "Don't even think about it." At that moment, common sense won out.

"Enticing as that offer sounds, I'll pass," I said, a slight smile on my face.

He moved a few steps closer, his altitudinous stature causing me to strain my neck. He smelled good, like Egyptian Musk.

"Are you sure?"

The look he was giving me with those honey-colored eyes of his was so sexy, seductive, and hypnotizing, I found myself about to give into his charms. I looked down at his penis that was now standing in full salute, then all the way back up to his handsome face. A few more seconds and Diego could have done with me whatever he wanted—that was, until I heard his phone buzz. It was sitting on the desk. I could see the name of the caller. It was Ricki. The name I could have sworn I heard him say early this morning when he was on the phone.

I smirked at him, saying, "Oh yeah, so sure. You might want to get that."

Diego looked from me to his phone. Seeing he had no chance of getting me in the shower, or anywhere else for that matter, he answered the phone.

"Hello," he said, sounding annoyed. He adjusted himself in his shorts and walked toward the door, leaving me shaking my head.

Walking into the bathroom, I looked in the mirror, noticing all the passion marks Diego had left on various parts of my body. I was hoping the ones on my neck would fade by the time I had to go to work on Tuesday. Didn't need anybody in my business.

After I turned on the shower, I put on the shower cap I found on the bathroom counter next to the bottles of hotel lotion, shampoo, and conditioner. When the water felt just right, I stepped into the tub. I used the little bar of hotel soap to wash my face, then lathered up a washcloth. The water felt good running down my back. It was warm and comforting.

I took deep cleansing breaths trying to clear my mind of everything, but try as I might, my thoughts kept wandering back to Diego. I still couldn't believe I slept with him, let alone on the first night of meeting him. Here I was, thirty-nine years old, acting like some college kid on spring break. I didn't even act like that when I was in college.

Yes, Diego was very appealing to the eye, charming, smart, and funny, but he was also arrogant, egotistical, and way too sure of himself. Definitely not the type of man I'd be involved with at all, not even for an occasional romp in the hay. Especially because I didn't do casual sex—until last night, that is. Maybe I was going through a midlife crisis. Or maybe it was simply because I hadn't been with anyone in over a year and my hormones had gotten the better of me. Whatever it was, like I told Shell, I didn't regret it. Regardless, I wouldn't have to worry about it, nor Diego, after tomorrow.

I was still in the shower when he returned. I turned off the water, grabbing a large towel off the rack. Once I had dried off, I wrapped the towel around myself and stepped out of the shower.

Diego poked his head inside the bathroom.

"I got everything on your list. And I found a few things for you in the boutique. I hope you like them," he said, placing two bags on the counter. One was from the Palmetto Market, the other from the Omni Boutique.

"Thank you," I replied.

"You're welcome," he said, giving me my privacy.

Removing my towel and folding it neatly, I placed it on the floor. I used the deodorant, lotion, and baby powder that I found in the Palmetto Market bag. Curious to see what he had gotten from the boutique, I took everything out of the bag and saw that he had bought me a black sleep shirt that read "I lost my virginity on Hilton Head Island" printed in big light blue letters. I couldn't help but laugh when I saw it. He also bought a pair of black lace boyshorts, a black bandeau bra top with matching panties, two pairs of black socks, a turquoise tank top, and a turquoise and black tennis skirt. I had to give it to the man; he did have good taste. Just by looking at everything, I could tell he had chosen the correct sizes.

I pulled the price tags off of everything, then donned a pair of socks, the boyshorts, and the sleep shirt. I placed the other clothes and toiletries in one bag, while tossing my dirty clothes in the other. As I went to throw away the price tags, I realized how expensive everything was. If I wasn't desperate, I would have made Diego take it all back. As it stood, I had no choice but to use what he bought for me, but I would definitely be reimbursing him for all of it.

Carrying the bags out of the bathroom, I placed them next to the bedroom couch. Diego was lying on the king-size bed, hands behind his head, eyes closed. He had taken off his sneakers, as well as his shirt. I couldn't help but admire his perfectly sculpted arms and chest, not to mention his rock-hard abs. He looked as if he was asleep, his chest rising and falling slowly. I wouldn't be surprised, considering how little sleep we had both gotten. He must have heard me because his eyes opened.

"Sorry, didn't mean to wake you," I said.

"Wasn't sleeping," he replied, looking in my direction.

I sat down on the bed. "Cute," I said, pointing to the words on the sleep shirt, making us both laugh. "Thank you for buying all that stuff," I said. "But you really didn't have to spend all that money. I'm going to pay you back."

"No need," he replied.

"The things you bought fit perfectly. How did you know what sizes to get?"

"That was easy," he said. "I just asked the saleswoman where the pint-size section was," he teased.

"Screw you, Diego," I kidded, a smile on my face.

"Just say the word," he replied in a tone so sexy I had to divert my gaze from his, the heat rising in my cheeks. He had me feeling some type of way, and I was trying my best not to let anything else happen between us.

Sidestepping his comment, I replied, "I can't let you pay for all that. I don't have my checkbook on me now, but I promise you I will pay you back."

Diego shook his head. "Like I told you before, there's no need. Consider it my gift to you for the good company. You saved me from having to look at Carl's mug for most of the weekend," he said with a wink.

"Well, thank you," I said, laughing. "You're pretty good company yourself."

"I also wanted to thank you for what you did for me earlier," he said.

I could only assume he was referring to our stairwell sexcapade. "You're welcome. My method may have been unorthodox, but you have to admit, it was effective."

"Yes, *very* effective. I have to say, you surprised me. I did *not* see that coming," he remarked, a sly look on his face.

"Heck, I surprised myself. And for the record, I couldn't see you coming, but I most *definitely* felt it," I replied, pretending to fan myself.

That got a hearty laugh out of Diego. "Are you hungry?"

I know he was referring to food, but looking at his extremely fit physique I could think of something else that I was hungry for. I quickly pushed that thought away. I knew all too well how easy it was to get caught up in good sex. I had a firsthand view of that with Shell. Besides, the sex with Diego wasn't just good, it was phenomenal, so I definitely couldn't afford to let that happen to me.

"I'm starving," I said.

He got off the bed, picking up the room service menu. Sitting back down next to me, he said, "Pick whatever you want, and I'll call downstairs."

We both looked through the menu. When I told him I was starving, it wasn't a lie. I hadn't eaten much since breakfast. I made my selection, then, passing the menu to Diego, he made his. He also picked out a nice bottle of Moscato d'Asti.

Once he called in our order, the conversation turned back to the reason for Diego's earlier freak-out.

"I can't believe I panicked like a little bitch, and now you know I have an issue with being in total darkness. Aside from my parents, no one else knows, not even Carl."

He lay back down, looking up at the ceiling.

I had never personally seen anyone have a panic attack, not even in practice as a doctor, but I knew the signs. Even though I couldn't see Diego when the lights went out, I could hear the signs loud and clear. His speech was erratic; his breathing increased to the point where I thought he was going to hyperventilate. Turning toward him, I sat cross-legged on the bed. I stared at him for a moment, trying to choose my words carefully. There was nothing worse than a man whose pride was wounded. Scratch that; there was nothing worse than a *black* man whose pride was wounded.

"Diego, you had . . . a moment, based on a traumatic event from your childhood. Today just happened to be a trigger. It's like a form of posttraumatic stress. I get it. It's nothing to be ashamed of."

"Is that your professional psychological assessment, Doctor?" he asked, looking over at me, grinning.

Smiling back, I replied, "Why, yes, it is. Look," I said, seriousness in my tone, "it takes a strong man to admit something like that, especially to a stranger. Your secret is safe with me."

"Thank you," he responded.

We heard a knock at the door. "Hold that thought," he said, getting up from the bed, walking to the living room.

He asked who it was before opening it. Once he confirmed it was room service, he let the server in. The young man wheeled in a cart containing two covered plates, utensils wrapped in expensive-looking cloth napkins, the bottle of Moscato in an ice bucket, and two wineglasses.

The server handed Diego the bill. He looked it over carefully, then signed it. Taking his wallet out of his pocket, he pulled out some money, handing it, along with the bill, to the server. After the young man thanked him repeatedly for what I assumed was a generous tip, they said their good-byes, and he left.

"Would you prefer to eat in the bedroom or out here in the living room?" Diego asked, just loud enough for me to hear him.

"In here is fine," I responded.

He wheeled the cart into the bedroom, positioning it so we could both reach it. He removed the covers from both plates, revealing the mouthwatering food. Not only did it look delicious, it smelled wonderful. Diego removed the cork from the Moscato, poured us both a glass, then recorked the bottle.

I didn't even wait for Diego to start eating I was that hungry. "You sure you're going to eat all that?" he asked.

"Watch me," I said, finishing off my crab cake, then tearing into my main course. "And if I'm still hungry, I might eat some of yours."

He raised an eyebrow. "I would ask where you put it all, but I think I already know."

"And where would that be?" I questioned.

"That pretty ass of yours that you claim I can't help but look at," he teased. Diego was savoring his food, taking his time with it, just like he did with me last night.

I laughed with him. "Hey, better there than anywhere else," I countered.

"You'll get no complaints from me," he noted in agreement. "I would ask you if you liked the food, but since you're almost done, I would take that as a yes."

I nodded. "You would be correct. And yours?" I asked, eyeing his filet mignon.

"It's good. Would you like to try some?"

I did, but not wanting to appear greedy, I simply replied in ladylike fashion, "No, thanks, I'm good."

Diego's phone, which was on the bed next to him, began to vibrate. It was close enough for me to see the name of the caller. It was Ricki again. I looked at him, a sly smile on my face.

"What?" he asked, letting the call go to voice mail as he finished his meal.

"Nothing," I coyly replied.

"That look didn't say nothing."

He got up, put the ice bucket with the wine and our glasses on the nightstand, and rolled the cart into the living room. He came back and stretched out on the bed, waiting for me to respond.

I made myself comfortable and lay on my stomach, my elbows resting on the bed. "It's just that for someone who's not your wife or girlfriend, she's called you a lot. Which leads me to believe you two have 'a thing,'" I said, making air quotes.

Looking at me questioningly, he asked, "'A thing'?" mimicking my hand motions.

"Yes, 'a thing.' You two aren't in a relationship, but you have an agreement of sorts."

"Is that another one of your expert assessments?"

He refilled both glasses, handing me mine.

"No, just the assessment from a woman who's been in more than one relationship over the years. I'm no longer involved with my ex, Daniel, but he still calls and texts me at times like we are."

Diego took a few sips of wine.

"Like when he called you last night?"

"I was wondering how much you'd heard," I replied.

"Sorry, I wasn't eavesdropping. But I did hear enough to know that he showed up at your home unexpectedly, was trying to monopolize your time, and was trying to make you feel guilty because you were away."

"Not eavesdropping, huh?" I needled.

He laughed, but then his voice took on a serious tone.

"I know you said he wasn't, but are you sure he's not crazy?"

"Daniel's harmless," I said, downplaying his question. "I was with him long enough to know he's more bark than bite. Anyway, I won't have to deal with him for another couple of days."

"Why deal with him at all?"

I shrugged. "Because even though we're not together, I'm still trying to be a good friend."

"Sometimes being a good friend means knowing when to let go and learning to let someone make their own way," he countered.

He did have a valid point. I wondered if he'd take his own advice. And as if on cue, his phone started to vibrate yet again.

"Aren't you going to answer that? It could be important," I said.

He picked up the phone, as if to answer it. Instead, he turned it off, placing it back on the nightstand. "It wasn't important," he replied.

I studied his face and could tell he had something on his mind.

"What is it?" I asked.

"You're leaving tomorrow," he stated.

"Yes."

"Can I be honest with you?"

"Absolutely. I wouldn't expect anything less."

"This may sound rude, but I want to be inside you right now."

Although I was a bit surprised by his candor, I couldn't fault the man for his honesty or his directness. "Tell me how you really feel," I said.

"If you allow me, I can show you better than I can tell you."

"I don't know, Diego. I think I've indulged a little too much already."

"Then what's one more indulgence? I promise, you won't be disappointed."

He leaned over, his lips meeting mine. He pulled me on top of him, his manhood pressing against me. Despite my misgivings, I succumbed to temptation. It was going to be our last time together, after all. My lips parted as his tongue entered my mouth, the sweet taste of wine still on his breath.

He reached under my sleep shirt, pulled it up and over my head, and tossed it to the side. Chest to chest, the fingers of one of his hands grabbed at my locs, the other at my boyshorts. He couldn't get them off fast enough. Just like my shirt earlier, he ripped them from my body. His big hands palmed my cheeks, squeezing them. I moaned into his mouth.

I sucked on his neck, trailing soft kisses down his chest, reaching his shorts. I got them, along with his boxer briefs, down halfway, freeing him from their constriction. He kicked them off the rest of the way. I took him in my hand, stroking him from shaft to tip, his precome coating my fingers. He groaned low and deep in his throat as I licked his head, lowering my mouth onto it. I brought him further into my mouth, his tip hitting the back of my throat. He inhaled and exhaled slowly, as his eyes rolled into the back of his head, his fingers digging into the sheets.

While I continued to orally pleasure him, Diego reached out for me, turning me around, lifting me up and lowering me until my sultry folds were in his face. He spread my lips with his fingers, penetrating me with his tongue. Wrapping his arms around my back, he held me in place, as we found sixty-nine ways to please each other.

Wanting to grant his request, I slid down his torso, grabbing a condom off the nightstand. Opening it, I sheathed him, turned myself around, and lowered myself slowly onto his penis, clenching my muscles along the way. I placed my hands on his chest, riding him, his fingernails digging into my thighs. I saw the sweet agony on his face as he tried to hold back. Grasping me firmly, he flipped me over onto my back, placing one of my legs on his shoulder; long, deep thrusts stroked my G-spot.

My soprano cries mixed with his deep bass ones until they culminated into a crescendo louder than the waves crashing outside as we climaxed in unison . . . The first of many, as we tasted, teased, and pleased each other from late night until early morning, until finally, we both collapsed in sweet exhaustion.

There was a warm breeze coming off of the ocean. The waves were calm and inviting, not like the choppy, harsh ones of just a few short hours ago. The sun was shining, and there wasn't a cloud in the sky. It was a perfect Sunday, my last full day in Georgia.

Diego and I decided to have breakfast together at HH Prime, sitting on the covered deck. We called Shell and Carl to let them know our plans but decided not to wait for them. Not that they had shown up yet anyway. It appeared that those two had lost their minds and seemed to have forgotten they were married—not to each other, but to other people.

"I hope those two get here soon," I said, biting into my Belgian waffle topped with bananas, strawberries, and whipped cream. "We have to get back on the road soon."

Diego was chowing down on two scrambled eggs with a prime cut five-ounce filet and golden potatoes. "No telling with those two. I know Carl's going through something, but I never expected this."

I nodded in agreement. "I never expected this from Shell either."

But then again, I was surprised by my own behavior. I seemed to have zoned out for a few seconds. The sound of Diego's voice brought me out of my trance.

"What?" I asked.

"I said you kept me up all night . . . again," he said with a wink.

"Are you complaining?"

"Never."

"You want me to apologize?" I teased.

"You could, but I wouldn't accept." We smiled at each other.

"Damn, y'all couldn't wait for us?" I heard Shell's voice behind me, breaking my flirtatious mood.

Turning around, I said, "We called the two of you over an hour ago, and you said you'd be down in ten minutes."

"Yeah, about that—"

Cutting her off I said, "Don't even. Whatever you're getting to eat, please get it to go. I want to get back on the road before traffic gets bad."

Diego had excused himself. He and Carl were off to the side talking. Shell ordered French toast with cinnamon and vanilla, with two side orders: fresh fruit and turkey bacon. She completed her order with a large cup of orange juice.

"Diego looks tired," she said, looking in his direction.

"We talked most of the night. The storm kept us up."

She looked at me skeptically, "Talked. Yeah, okay."

Her food arrived quickly, allowing me to avoid her further scrutiny, for the moment, anyway. After Carl picked up her tab, they walked us to our car. I had already placed my bags in the car before breakfast. Opening the trunk, Carl put Shell's belongings inside. Once she put her food on the front passenger seat and her orange juice in a cup holder, she and Carl stepped to the side to say their good-byes. They were kissing and hugging like she was his brand-new bride and he was going off to war.

Diego and I moved to the rear of the vehicle. "Well, this is it," I said. "I actually had a nice time," I stated, looking up at him.

"Me too," he replied. "But don't let it go to your head," he teased, making light of yesterday's conversation.

"Me? Never," I said.

Diego leaned down, kissing me on the cheek. He smiled at me. "You have a safe trip back home, Gabrielle."

I returned his smile. "You too. And get some sleep."

We waved to each other as he and Carl headed back to the hotel. Shell was standing there, her arms crossed in front of her, looking at me the way she does one of her children when they are caught doing something wrong.

I walked to the driver's side, climbed into the vehicle, fastened my seat belt, and waited for her to do the same. She took her food off the seat, placed it on her lap, then fastened her seat belt.

"Hmph," she said.

"What?" I asked, placing the key in the ignition.

"*Talked,* my ass!" she said, shaking her head.

As I drove off, all I could do was laugh. The weekend didn't turn out at all like I expected, but in the end, I was left with some very fond memories of my weekend affair.

Epilogue

Part I: Carl

It was the third Saturday in March, March fifteenth, to be exact. I had always set the third Saturday of the month aside like clockwork to have lunch with my mom; a time I set aside to make sure all of her needs were taken care of. Even though I paid most of her monthly expenses through automatic bill pay, I still wanted to make sure that she didn't need or want for anything else.

Usually, it was just the two of us in order for Mom and me to spend some quality time together, but on this outing, I invited my younger sister Anastasia. Graduation was fast approaching, and I wanted to know what she wanted for her graduation gift. When it came to graduations, I always let my siblings choose their reward. They put in all the hard work, so they deserved that option.

I was now permanently living at the two-bedroom condo Dalisay and I owned in Chelsea in Manhattan. I still had some things I needed from the house, so I decided to kill two birds with one stone . . . pick up my belongings and take Mom to her favorite restaurant in Garden City, Seasons 52. She loved the food there because all of the items on the menu were less than 475 calories.

You see, Mom was, let's just say a *big* lady, and she loved her soul food. If wasn't for me making sure she had healthy food in her home, no telling how or what she would eat. Not to mention she was very sedentary. She was tall, standing at about five feet ten, but she also weighed about 250 pounds. In her younger days, she reminded me the late actress Tamara Dobson, who portrayed Cleopatra Jones in the 1970s Blaxploitation movies. But that was then; this is now. Recently, she had a doctor's appointment that scared the life out of her. Her blood pressure was elevated, she was borderline diabetic, and her cholesterol and triglycerides were high. I think the doctor put the fear of God in her because she called me in a panic saying she needed to make major changes in her lifestyle. She even asked me to help her get a gym membership.

The doctor told her that she needed to change her diet and start exercising or else she was running the risk of cutting quite a few years off her life, which would scare anyone, especially since she was only fifty-five. Funny thing is, I had been telling her the same exact thing for years. Guess because I didn't have MD after my name I didn't know what the hell I was talking about.

The plan was for me to pick up Mom and Ana from Mom's three-bedroom Harlem condo, and to head to Garden City from there. After that, we'd quickly shoot over to the house. I was hoping Dali wouldn't be there. Neither Mom nor Ana were particularly fond of her, especially now. If I was completely honest with myself, I'd finally have to admit that Mom never liked her. Like Diego, Mom thought she was a gold digger. I remember plenty of times when we would visit Mom when we were in college, and would get severely clowned by both of them. But unlike Diego, Mom was too nice to say, "I told you so."

I was fortunate enough to live someplace that had an attached indoor parking deck. Many people in the city weren't as lucky. Some parked on the street, having to

deal with alternate-side-of-the-street parking regula-
tions, while others parked their cars in parking decks,
paying exorbitant amounts of money monthly to keep
their cars safe. I was from New York and many people,
including myself, have cars and take public transporta-
tion.

Once I got to my car, I called Ana to make sure she was
already at Mom's.

"Hey, Panther," I heard my little sis say.

"Hey, Nu'bia," I replied.

As kids, Ana and I were avid comic book readers.
Aside from the fact that we loved to read, I figured we
were so into comics because a fantasy world seemed
much better than our reality as we knew it. She called me
Panther, short for Marvel Comics Black Panther, and her
nickname was Nu'bia after the black Amazonian warrior
from DC Comics. Even though we were adults, the names
still stuck, especially for Ana, who looked like an Amazon
standing at six feet. She always kept her hair in either
an Afro or in braids, and looked even more like Tamara
Dobson, who was six feet two.

"I'm on my way. Are you two ready?"

"Yeah, Mom's picking out a wig to wear, and you know
how long that takes, but other than that, we're ready."

I shook my head. Mom had more wigs at home than
Vivica Fox had in her wig line. "Okay, well, traffic is
good, so I'll be there in about fifteen minutes."

"All right, just call me when you're out front."

"Will do."

On the short drive uptown, I thought about last month's
trip to Savannah, about Shell, and wondered how she was
faring. I thought about how I had no remorse whatsoever
for what happened between us. Like I kept telling myself,
once Dalisay cheated and decided to keep dude's baby,

our marriage was officially over. Although we were married on paper, in my heart, it was a done deal.

I still had Shell's phone number but decided against contacting her. Her life seemed complicated enough as it was, and I didn't want to add to it. Besides, even if I did want to continue seeing her, there was no telling if she had gotten back with her husband. Although she sounded doubtful at the time, she hadn't completely ruled out reconciling with the jackass. Then there was the distance. Atlanta was almost 900 miles away, and although I could easily hop a flight on a whim to see Shell, she didn't have it like that. Between taking care of her kids and going school, she probably wouldn't have any time at all for me. And let's not forget, she was only twenty-six years old. Although she said she liked older men, she still married someone her own age. Makes me wonder if she could truly handle being with someone more mature. While I enjoyed our short time together, all things considered, realistically, at this moment, I couldn't envision there being an "us."

I did have to admit, though, that was some good motherfuckin' pussy. Even after two kids, it still had that snapback. I guess that comes from being young, but my old forty-year-old ass showed her a thing or two. Had her screaming my name and coming all over the place. Even got her to admit her husband never hit like I did. Yes, I do have a bit of an ego. Dali shot it to hell in a few months with all her bullshit, but it took less than forty-eight hours with Shell to remind me who I truly was—the motherfuckin' man. I would definitely consider making a special trip just to be in the middle of those thick thighs again. My dick got hard just thinking about it.

About fifteen minutes later, I arrived at Mom's. I pushed all thoughts of Shell to the back of my mind and called Ana. She and Mom came downstairs and hopped into the car. Once pleasantries were exchanged, I drove the short thirty minutes to Seasons 52. Conversation was kept to small talk, the main discussion being held for the restaurant.

Once we were seated, I began. "Mom, all the bills for the month have been paid. Is there anything else you want or need?"

"No, Bert," she said, making me cringe.

I hated that nickname, especially when she used it in public. She had been calling me that for years. Said it was because even as a baby, I was so serious and always had my brows furrowed, like the character from Sesame Street.

"Now, Mommy, you know Panther hates when you call him that," Ana said, laughing.

"Well, if he would stop being so serious all the time and smile a bit more, maybe I'd stop calling him that," she said with a wink.

"You know he's going through some things, and I doubt he feels like smiling much these days. Cut him some slack."

"Hell, he should be grinning from ear to ear, knowing he'll be rid of the bitch from hell soon. That's reason enough to smile," she countered, looking over the menu. Mom was not one to mince words.

"I'm right here, you know," I said, a scowl on my face.

Mom patted me on the hand. She always did that when she wanted me to calm down, wanted to comfort me.

"We know, Bert. I just want you to be happy. You missed out on a lot when you were a child because of me, and now, you'll soon get the opportunity to live your life. That's something to be happy about; that, and the fact that you're alive, successful, and have a great career. Those are things to be grateful for."

I couldn't argue with her. Nor could I deny the fact that I couldn't be upset with her for too long. She always knew how to get to me.

"You're right, Mom, and I am grateful."

At that moment, our waiter showed up, ready to take our orders. Mom ordered organic steamed edamame as an appetizer, and as her entrée, an organic baby spinach salad with raspberries, toasted pine nuts, goat cheese, and white balsamic vinaigrette. For a drink, she simply ordered water with lemon, much to the shock of Ana and me. Being from the South, Mom loved her sweet tea. We both gave each other a look after Mom completed her order.

"Now, don't go giving each other those side looks like you always do. I know I have to eat better. I ain't tryin' to die no time soon," she said a smile on her face.

"Mom, you know we're just concerned, that's all," I said.

I stopped speaking so Ana could place her order; then I placed mine. We both chose water as our beverage in support of Mom and her healthy lifestyle change.

"Mommy, we're just happy you're taking this so seriously and want you to know we will fully support you in any way we can."

"Well, I appreciate the support, but don't go changing your ways for me. This is something I need to do, not you."

"You may not want our full support, but you've got it anyway, whether you like it or not," I said, adjusting my glasses.

"Boy, you better watch that tone," Mom said, pointing a finger at me. "I know you're used to running things, including other people's lives, but I got this. Understood?"

"Yes, ma'am," I said taking a sip of water from my glass.

Mom was the only person on the planet who could get away with calling me "boy." Anybody else would get chin checked. She was right though; I was used to controlling the situations and people in my life, but that was out of habit more than anything else. I had noticed recently that she had started to take more control of her life, and while I thought it was a good thing, I still liked being in charge.

"Okay, did you get a chance to look into the gym membership for me?" she asked.

As our food was being placed on the table, I replied, "Yes. I checked with your insurance company, and as part of a wellness incentive, you are entitled to use certain gyms free of charge. The closest one to you is the YMCA right around the corner. It has senior classes, a pool, personal trainers, everything you need. If you want, I can go with you to help you sign up."

"That would be appreciated. Thank you, Carl."

I shifted my attention to Ana. "I wanted to know what you wanted for your graduation gift, Ms. Ph.D.," I said with pride. She wasn't my child, but I still felt like a proud poppa. Ana was the smartest of us all, even me, and that's something that was hard to admit.

She stopped eating to answer me. "I was thinking maybe a down payment for a flat across the pond?" She looked a bit scared as she asked.

I gazed at her, a quizzical look on my face. "Why would you need a place in England?"

She looked from Mom to me. "Because I've been offered a teaching position there, and I really want to accept it. It's a once-in-a-lifetime opportunity."

Mom jumped up from her seat, reaching over to give Ana a huge bear hug. "Baby, I am *so* proud of you. But there was no doubt in my mind that you'd do great things, just like your brother over there."

I too was proud of Ana, but at the same time, I couldn't imagine her not being close to the family. She'd be all alone, in a foreign country, with no one looking out for her, no Panther to have her back. Not to mention I was losing my road dog. But I had to realize my little sister was a grown woman who had to make her own decisions and live her life on her own terms. All I could do was be happy for her, and be there if and when she needed me.

"Nu'bia, you got it."

She raised one eyebrow. "Hold up. No argument? No trying to convince me to stay? Who are you, and what did you do with my Panther?" she teased.

I laughed. "Panther had to learn to let Nu'bia be her own woman. You've grown into a pretty amazing one at that. Just promise me two things."

"What's that?" she asked.

"One, you let me throw you the biggest, most bad-ass graduation party ever, and two, you allow me to provide you with an open ticket so you can come home whenever you want."

This time it was Ana's turn to get up. "You got it, big bro," she said, kissing me on the cheek.

Once we finished eating, we drove to the house, which took no time at all. I parked the car in the driveway, waiting for Mom and Ana to get out. I knew Dalisay was there because her car was also in the driveway. I couldn't worry about that now. I just wanted to get my belongings and go.

When I got to the door, I tried my key. It wouldn't turn. I thought maybe the lock was frozen because of the frigid temperatures, so I tried opening the side door to the garage, and then I used my garage door opener. None of them worked. That bitch had all the locks changed! I felt myself getting pissed. How the fuck was she going to change the locks on a house that had my goddamn name on the deed?

I rang the doorbell, waiting for her to answer. No reply. I called both the house phone and her cell phone, and still no response. Finally, when I started banging on the door threatening to call the police because she locked me out of my own home, she reluctantly answered.

"What do you want, Carl?" she sneered.

"What the fuck do I want? What do you mean what the fuck do I want?" I questioned, pushing past her, with Ana and Mom right behind me. "This is still *my* motherfuckin' house, and I can come and go as I please. Who gave you the right to change the goddamn locks?"

"You haven't been here since your trip last month. *That's* what gave me the right."

As she stood there, I noticed for the first time her baby bump. She was about four months pregnant, and she had no problem showing it off dressed in a tee shirt and some leggings. Looking at her disgusted me.

"Bitch, you have no right!" I yelled. "I own most of this house, not to mention most of the shit in this house. Now get those locks changed back immediately, or else," I said, looking down at her.

"Or else *what,* Carl? Are you going to grab me up again like the last time? Or maybe you'll sic your entourage on me," she said, nodding in the direction of Mom and Ana.

"Hey, don't bring me into your hot ghetto mess," Ana replied.

"Why are you here then? Get the fuck out of my house."

Ana was usually the more levelheaded peacemaker of the family. She always looked to diffuse a situation rather than light the match. The exception came when someone attacked a family member. That's when the claws came out.

"Look here, Dalisay, I'm here for my brother, the man who put up the majority of the funds for this palatial abode of yours, so, in reality, this is *his* house. If it wasn't for Carl, you wouldn't have this house in the first place. So I suggest you stand down and let him get his stuff."

Ana had a way of getting her point across, yet still sounding eloquent at the same time—unlike Mom or me, who were crass as hell and didn't give a fuck. Dalisay couldn't verbally tangle with Ana, so she went for the next available target . . . Mom.

"And why did you bring your mother? This simple-minded bitch isn't good for much of anything."

Damn, and I actually *married* this disrespectful bitch? What did I ever see in her? I guess her true colors were finally showing. "Dalisay, talk about my mom again and it's over."

"What, you don't want me to talk about how this stupid, ignorant whore had six bastard kids by five different men? Or how about the fact that she didn't even finish high school? It's a wonder any of you even finished, considering who your mother was. I knew she never liked me, but guess what, Betty Jean? I never liked you either," she said, pure venom in her tone.

"By the way, Carl," she continued, "that was one thing I really couldn't stand about you; how you felt the need to take care of everybody in your fucking family. You spent tens of thousands of dollars on them . . . money that could have been spent elsewhere. Claimed you wanted your family to have the best opportunities money could buy. Thing is, you did it on your own, so why couldn't they? I wanted to leave New York years ago, but because of them, you wouldn't leave. *I* was your wife. *I* should have come first. And for the record, I wanted to have a child, just not with you. I was afraid the stupid gene would rub off."

The bitch had already crossed a line talking about my mom. She knew what my mom had been through growing up, and now she was using it against her. And she was trying to make it seem like she got nothing while my family got everything. But when she mentioned why she didn't want to have my child, it seemed as if someone had taken over my body. As I stepped toward her, I saw fear in Dalisay's eyes. I was ready to put my hands around her neck; that was, until Mom stepped in front of me.

"It's okay, son, I've got this," she said, putting her hands on her my shoulders, again calming me down. Ana reached out to me, pulling me further away from Dalisay, who was still within arm's reach.

Mom was country ghetto and knew how to scrap physically as well as verbally, so I stepped off, allowing her to handle Dalisay. Turning to face her, Mom put her hands on her oversized hips, saying, "Let me tell you something, Miss Wannabe High Society Bourgeois Gold Digging Tramp. I will admit I've made a lot of mistakes, least of which was not being the best mother to my children, but at least I never lied, cheated, nor have I made goddamn excuses for my bad life choices.

"My son is a damn good man, definitely *too* good for the likes of a no-account piece of shit like you. He took care of his family because, unlike you, he believes in family. You would have been damn lucky for him to be the father of your child. You've ridden his gravy train for over seventeen long goddamn years. He took care of your trifling ass and took care of *your* fuckin' family too. He gave you the world, and you gave him your stankin' ass to kiss, you skanky piece of gutter trash. Yeah, you may have a little money doin' what you do, and I may not be the smartest person out there, but I *am* smart enough to know that your net worth is *nothing* compared to Carl's. He can buy and sell your silly ass several times over.

"And you have the fuckin' nerve to call me a stupid, ignorant whore? You, the dumb ass who cheated on her husband, fucked another man, and got pregnant by him? *You're* the one who's carrying a bastard child. So now, who's the stupid, ignorant whore? And let me tell you something else; you may, by some chance, get your baby daddy to marry you, but mark my words, you keep 'em how you get 'em. So good luck with that, bitch. Guess it's true what they say . . . You can't turn a ho into a housewife."

All I could do was stand there in awe. I can honestly admit that I was genuinely proud of my mother; proud of her for the way she handled Dalisay, proud of her for owning up to her mistakes, and proud of her for standing up for me the way she did. Mom walked up to Dalisay, standing directly in front of her.

"And one more thing," she said.

Next thing I knew, Mom had pulled her hand back like a slingshot bitch-slapping Dalisay square across the face. She slapped her so hard, Dali flew across the room. When she steadied herself, I saw the imprint left by Mom's fingers.

"I've wanted to slap that smug taste out of your mouth for years. How ya like me now, hooker?" Mom said, heading toward the front door, her chest puffed out. Ana just shook her head, following behind Mom.

"I'll expect those locks to be changed back no later than Monday." I turned on my heel, leaving Dalisay in shock, holding her cheek, leaning against a wall. If Mom wanted me to smile more, that display just earned her one at the very least.

A few hours later and I was still fuming. I had dropped off Mom and Ana, but was still angry. Mom wanted me to stay with them for a while until I cooled off; afraid I was going to go back to the house. She made me promise that I wouldn't, and she knew I would keep my word.

Instead of going there, I drove to Brooklyn, intending to hang at Diego's place. I called him, only to find out that he was at his parents' house in Queens. He told me to wait for him, so I parked my car, then walked to one of the bars we frequented. It was right up the block from Diego. By the time he got there, I was in seven shots of tequila deep, and that was after three beers. Diego had the bartender cut me off, paid my tab, and made me walk back to his condo.

"Can you believe that shit?" I said, after filling him in. I had plopped down on the oversized leather couch in the living room.

"Yeah, Miss Betty Jean called me after you did. She gave me the play-by-play while I was driving home. Dalisay is really a piece of work. But I told you that a long time ago, and you refused to listen."

I threw up my hands. "Here you go again." Diego was on his "I told you so" bullshit, but I allowed him continue.

"Look, man, do you want a friend or a yes-man, because you know I'm never going to lie to you nor tell you what you want to hear? So here it is straight, no chaser; stop acting brand new like you're surprised by her actions. I told you from the beginning you shouldn't have gotten involved with Dalisay, let alone married her. I told you she was a gold digger. That woman didn't give you the time of day until she found out about your internship and job offer from Apple.

"Hell, even Miss Betty Jean warned you about her time and again, but because she was your mom, and you had problems with her, you tuned her out. Because of your fuckin' Mommy issues, you chased after Dalisay and a host of other non-black females on campus; anyone who *didn't* remind you of your mom in some way.

"And it's funny because you had some of the most beautiful, intelligent sistas feeling you; some of them much hotter and way smarter than Dalisay, but because of their race—*your* race—you wouldn't give them the time of day. You claimed you liked Dalisay because of her ambition, but some of those women were just as ambitious, if not more so. And what did you call them? Too independent for their own damn good. Now, you see, Dalisay took ambition to a whole new level, and you're mad as fuck. While I sympathize with you, bro, don't be salty now because I was right."

Damn this smug motherfucker! I came here looking for some support, not another lecture on why I never dated black women, and definitely not another lecture on why I shouldn't have married Dali.

"You know what, man, I don't need this," I said, pretty sure I was slurring my words. "But while we're being so honest with each other, *bro*, here's some truth for you. Don't act like your ass is an expert on women, because you're not. You think you've got Ricki right where you want her, and she's okay with your arrangement. But I'm here to tell you, she's not. That little girl only stays around because she's in love with you. Mark my words, that shit's gonna come back to bite you in the ass one day."

Diego had a smirk on his face. "That day will never come because Ricki and I are about to be done."

I looked at him, raising an eyebrow. "Why? Has your child paramour finally wised up, or are just tired of her like all of the other women you've discarded over the years?" He didn't answer. "And speaking of all your past bed buddies, let's talk about the reason why your ass can't commit to any woman."

"Let's not," he said. I could tell he was pissed off, but I didn't give a fuck.

"You can tell me about my epic relationship failure, but I can't return the favor? Negro, please! I warned *you* from the jump that Carmelita was a ho of a first-class nature. Hell, she was passed around more than a joint at a reggae concert. You knew I even tapped that.

"But no, you thought you could make an honest woman out of that tramp; called yourself catchin' feelings and shit. And how did that work out for you? Oh wait . . . It didn't. She cheated on your ass. Had you crying like a little bitch. And even after you dropped her like the bad habit she was, you still went on banging her—why, I have no idea. She fucked you up so badly, you can't even be in a meaningful relationship. You may not be able to admit it, but Carmelita still controls your ass. You think you're being honest with all the women you've been with, but really, you're just making sad, sorry excuses for why you hit and run. So don't preach to me about how I treat black women, because, dude, you ain't no prize either."

"You done?" he asked, anger in his eyes. If I didn't know better, I would have thought he wanted to hit me.

"Yeah," I replied.

"Well, let me set you straight on a few things. First of all, Carmelita did *not* have me crying like *a little bitch,* as you so eloquently put it," he said, sarcasm oozing from his tone. "Second, at least I didn't try to wife her or have a kid with her, unlike you did with Dalisay. Now, I would throw your drunk ass out, but you can't drive right now. Plus, I wouldn't be your friend if I did put your ass out on the street. So keep your motherfuckin' ass on that couch, and sleep that shit off," he said, walking away from me.

Yeah, I had definitely hit a nerve. Otherwise, he would have let me sleep in one of the guest bedrooms. Oh-fuckin'-well, truth hurts. I kicked my shoes off, stretching out on the couch. Diego may not have wanted to talk to me, but I knew someone who would. Before I went to sleep, I sent a text message to the one person I knew would be glad to hear from me.

Epilogue

Part II: Mischelle

It had been a month. One month since I'd been to Tybee Island and almost two since my marriage had fallen apart. As crazy as it sounded, I came back from Tybee with the hopes that maybe there was something left of my marriage to salvage. I even prayed that it had all been one big nightmare. Malik's cheating, me and Carl . . . anything to put my life back the way it was before. But there was no nightmare. Only the cold reality that my family had been pulled apart.

Malik wasn't coming back. He had seriously walked out on me and the children, and there was nothing I could do about it. No matter how much I'd cried, begged, and pleaded, Malik didn't care. He had made up his mind that he was done. I never thought this would be us. After I got back home, things got worse. Malik no longer talked to me as if I was his wife. Malik and I had gotten into knock-down, drag-out fights. He threatened to take the children, and I told him it would be a cold day in hell. There had been some physical altercations, more so on his part than mine.

I struggled to pay bills. If it hadn't been for food stamps, the kids and I would go hungry. I think the worst part of it all, the part that sickened me the most, was when I found out Malik had been taking money from home and spending it on the side girl. He hadn't been paying the car note as I thought he was. I didn't find that out until the dealership called me with a threat to repossess the car. It took me *six hours* to finally get in contact with Malik—only for him to act as if I had no right to question him.

I tried to be the bigger person in our situation, but Malik wouldn't let me. He would take the car and stay the night at Janay's house. He knew we had to take the children to school daily but each morning, he would show up late to do so. I shed tears because it became more apparent to me that my husband had little to no respect for me, our children, or our home.

As the days went on, I could hardly pretend nothing was wrong. Professor Hall picked up on the fact that I was going through something.

"You wear your emotions on your face. Did you know that?" he'd asked one day after one of our mock trial sessions at the courthouse.

Those sessions were my favorite thing about his criminal law and justice class. I got to live out my fantasy of being a lawyer and breaking down the ins and outs of the criminal justice system. Professor Hall wore glasses and had locs too. I said too because I couldn't help but think of Carl from time to time when I looked at the professor. My body heated up at the thought of the man who I'd shared my weekend affair with.

"I've heard it before, a time or two," I answered him.

He smiled down at me. "Is there anything I can do to help?"

I shook my head. "I doubt it. I'm just stressed. Things going on at home."

I checked my phone again. Malik had told me he would pick me up since he refused to leave the car with me. But I'd been sitting on those steps outside the courthouse for almost an hour. All of my classmates had gone home, so I'd missed any chance of getting a ride with them. Professor Hall took a seat beside me. He laid his brown leather carrying case on the step in front of him, and then gazed out over the parking lot before looking back at me.

"Is that the reason you're sitting out here on these steps? I've been waiting on you to leave for a while. I'm not going to leave you sitting out here by yourself," he told me.

"Oh, you don't have to do that. My hus—Malik said he would pick me up."

I felt bad that he had been waiting on me before he would go home.

"Does he know what time class ended?"

"He does."

"You know, when you mentioned his name you cringed. Not to mention I notice your wedding set is no longer on your finger."

Damn, he was observant, I thought. I'd sold my rings so I could pay the electric bill for the month. Had been walking through the mall and the lady at a booth that boasted of buying gold asked me if I wanted to sell my rings. I got seventy-five bucks for the whole set. That money went right to Georgia Power. I was about to try to deny everything, but before I knew it, my tears betrayed me.

I could feel the professor watching me, but he was smart enough not to say anything for a while. Then he wrapped an arm around my shoulders.

"You're a smart young woman, Mischelle. One of the brightest students I've had in my classes for a long time. I'm not going to tell you you're strong because right now, you aren't. You're hurting, and this kind of pain is the hardest in the world to deal with. You feel like a failure. You're wondering when your marriage slipped away from you."

I looked over at him through my tears. I had to wonder if he had been in a situation similar to what I was going through because he was hitting all the nails on their heads.

"It burns me up inside so bad," I told him, my sobs flowing in earnest.

"I know. I went through a divorce last year. I felt your pain a mile away because it was familiar to mine."

"Does it ever get better?" I asked as the wind whipped around us.

He nodded once. "In time it does. But until then, cry when need to, but never let him break your spirit. Okay? Sometimes the Most High closes one door so he can open many more." He stood, then offered me his hand so I could stand. "Come on. Let me take you home."

I wanted to tell him he didn't have to, but I could pretty much figure out that Malik wasn't coming at this point. On the drive home, he told me if I needed help with my divorce, he knew someone who could help me.

"I can't afford an attorney," I told him after he parked in front of my apartment.

"Don't worry about that. Just let me know if you need help," he responded.

I smiled. So did he, and for a moment, I swore he was Carl all over again. I wouldn't say it was because they looked alike, but more so because of the knight-in-shining-armor similarities. I thanked him, then made my way inside.

Needless to say, Malik never showed up. My mother had picked up the kids from day care like she always did on Fridays. The one thing I didn't want to hear was a lecture from her, but I knew I was going to get one. So I prepared myself. She walked into my apartment with her nose turned in the air and eyes roaming as always. She had on a long black skirt and a simple white blouse. Black flats adorned her feet, and her hair sat in a bun. Her almond butter complexion glowed naturally.

"A lady never goes to bed with a dirty house," she told me.

"I'm cleaning now," I drably replied.

"What's going on with you and Malik? What's this mess all about?"

"Malik is mad because he wants me to be something I'm not. So he decided to find a young, hot-in-the-ass trollop to be what he wanted."

"A woman is supposed to be whatever her husband tells her to be. If he wants you to be his whore, then you be the nastiest God-fearing whore you can be. No marriage bed is defiled."

Her words pricked me like thorns as I walked through my home cleaning. Malik could do no wrong in her eyes. He was the best thing that had ever happened to me according to her. She was sitting at my kitchen table, preaching as I cleaned.

"You still going to school, I see. A married woman don't need all that education. You make that man feel less than he is talking about you doing that for the family. That's telling him you don't believe in him, trust in him enough to provide for his family."

I plopped down on my sofa. Dumped the clean laundry I'd done earlier to the floor so I could fold and put away clothes.

"That's the problem. Most new age women think they more man than the man they got at home. You keep a clean house. Keep them kids up while that man goes out and brings home the bacon. All that independent crap gon' leave you alone. I tried to tell you. A man shouldn't have to work, and then come to work some more. A good woman keeps her man well rested so he can go out into the workforce and make a living. Clean up after your husband. It's what any wife worth her weight in gold does. You doing too much, writing all that filth and taking classes. When you make time for that man you married?"

I swallowed back bile as I folded my kids' clothing.

"What about when that man isn't bringing in enough bacon? What about when he isn't doing enough to keep the home sustained?" I asked.

"Then you must be doing something wrong. When a man knows he got a good thang at home, he gon' make sure she suffers for nothing. You need to figure out what wrong you doing."

After a while, I tuned her out, like always. She must have picked up on it because she started to focus on the kids. I was so exasperated after she left, I was on the verge of tears. I picked my purse up from the end table and searched for my phone so I could call Gabby. I just needed her positivity in the moment. I found what I was looking for through the mess of receipts in my purse. I touched the power button at the top to see I had a text message.

I need to see you, it read.

My heart raced . . . body temperature shot up a notch.

Carl . . .

I hadn't heard from him since I left the island. The nights we spent together bum-rushed me. The tingling in my vagina wouldn't let up. I was flushed. He needed to see me? Why?

We both agreed that we'd leave our weekend affair as it was. As much as I'd thought about him over the past few weeks, I wouldn't dare call him. I didn't have the fortitude to reach back out to the man who'd helped me break my vows.

As crazy as it all sounded, I missed him. Missed the fantasy he was to me for two days. That craving he'd given me . . . the sex . . . the orgasms.

Carl *needed* to see me. I let that play around in my mind as I laid the phone down and started to fold clothes again. All thoughts of calling Gabby vanquished in the wind. It took me a good twenty minutes to make up my mind to text Carl back.

Why? I sent back to him.

Going through some shit. Drunk as shit too.

You're drunk?

I need to seeee yu.

*see you
I don't know how that's going to be possible.
Mak et possible.
Make it* he corrected again.

At that point, I knew he was drunk. Misspelling words as I was sure he'd be slurring them had we been talking. I didn't know why I got excited at the notion of seeing that man again. I knew damn well I shouldn't have even been toying with the idea. But Carl made me feel beautiful. He doted on me like I was the only woman in the world who mattered to him. I'd worn the sundress he'd bought for me to school the week before.

One day when he came to see the kids, Malik questioned where it had come from since he knew I had no money to buy anything new. I lied and told him Gabby had bought it. He called her all kinds of dyke bitches because he thought she'd purchased that sundress. I apologized to Gabby in spirit for dragging her into my mess. Malik had never been too fond of her.

You act like I can just up and leave, I sent to Carl.
I can send for you, he hit me back.
I can't leave my kids like that.

I waited for him to text back before I got up to put the clothes away. When he didn't after ten minutes, I finished cleaning. I didn't know why I was even entertaining the idea of hooking up with him again anyway. I had way too much shit going on, and I had to wonder if he had gotten his divorce yet.

I left my phone on my desk as thoughts of Carl danced in my head. I remembered the way his mouth had satisfied me in the shower back at the Omni. Remembered the way he'd entered me, filled me up to the hilt, and then some. As I washed away the day's hard work, I had to wonder if my unwillingness to just up and leave my kids behind to be with him had turned him off. So what if it had? I reasoned. He couldn't possibly think I was the kind of woman to neglect my children for a quick roll in the hay, could he?

I turned the shower off and wrapped myself in a clean bath towel. I didn't even feel like drying off. I walked into my bedroom, tossed the towel, then climbed in bed. The kids were down for the night, and I just needed a moment to breathe. I thought of Tybee Island. Thought of the sounds of rain and the ocean crashing against the shores as Carl had entered me. I thought of hard abs, a chiseled chest, a Colgate smile, aromatic spicy scents, and locs. Saw thin, black-framed glasses and liquid black eyes smiling down at me as chocolate skin glistened with sweat.

Damn . . . If only I could touch myself and get off the way Carl had gotten me off. As it was, I'd never been able to get myself off without help, so I got up, pulled on a night shirt, and headed back downstairs to make sure everything was locked up tight. The green light on my phone was flashing. I had several missed calls from Malik and a text from Carl. There would be no way I'd call Malik back after he'd left me stranded. For one, I knew all we would do was argue. And I wasn't in the mood tonight.

I'm coming to Atlanta, the message from Carl read.

I didn't know whether I should have been happy or scared. A combination of both emotions settled into my stomach. He was coming to Atlanta. I kept reading his text over and over again. I had no idea how this would turn out. Carl being in Atlanta had the potential to open up a whole other can of worms, one I wasn't sure I'd be able to contain.